A friendship on the rocks

"Hey guys, chill," Ned said now. "We're all teammates, remember?"

It was true, all five of them were on the town team, and sometimes they were the five on the court.

"Ned's right," Pedro said.

"And teammates are supposed to stick, right?" Ned said.

Then before Pedro or anybody else could agree with him on that, Ned Hancock said, "Even when they decide to run against each other."

Now he looked right at Pedro as if he were looking at him for the first time, as if he'd turned into a stranger.

"Right, Pete?" he said, grinning.

And in that moment, it was as if Ned was the one who had turned into a stranger.

Then Ned and his buds were out the double doors and gone.

OTHER BOOKS YOU MAY ENJOY

The Big Field	Mike Lupica
The Boy Who Saved Baseball	John H. Ritter
Free Baseball	Sue Corbett
Heat	Mike Lupica
Hot Hand	Mike Lupica
Million-Dollar Throw	Mike Lupica
Miracle on 49th Street	Mike Lupica
Over the Wall	John H. Ritter
The River Between Us	Richard Peck
Safe at Home	Mike Lupica
Samurai Shortstop	Alan Gratz
Stand Tall	Joan Bauer
Summer Ball	Mike Lupica
Travel Team	Mike Lupica
Two-Minute Drill	Mike Lupica
Under the Baseball Moon	John H. Ritter

LONG SHOT

a Comeback Kids novel

MIKE LUPICA

PUFFIN BOOKS
An Imprint of Penguin Group (USA) Inc.

WALDEN MEDIA®

PUFFIN BOOKS
Published by the Penguin Group
Penguin Young Readers Group, 345 Hudson Street, New York, New York 10014, U.S.A.
Penguin Group (Canada), 90 Eglinton Avenue East, Suite 700,
Toronto, Ontario, Canada M4P 2Y3 (a division of Pearson Penguin Canada Inc.)
Penguin Books Ltd, 80 Strand, London WC2R 0RL, England
Penguin Ireland, 25 St Stephen's Green, Dublin 2, Ireland (a division of Penguin Books Ltd)
Penguin Group (Australia), 250 Camberwell Road, Camberwell, Victoria 3124, Australia
(a division of Pearson Australia Group Pty Ltd)
Penguin Books India Pvt Ltd, 11 Community Centre,
Panchsheel Park, New Delhi - 110 017, India
Penguin Group (NZ), 67 Apollo Drive, Rosedale, North Shore 0632, New Zealand
(a division of Pearson New Zealand Ltd)
Penguin Books (South Africa) (Pty) Ltd, 24 Sturdee Avenue,
Rosebank, Johannesburg 2196, South Africa

Registered Offices: Penguin Books Ltd, 80 Strand, London WC2R 0RL, England

First published in the United States of America by Philomel Books,
a division of Penguin Young Readers Group, 2008
Published by Puffin Books, a division of Penguin Young Readers Group, 2010

1 3 5 7 9 10 8 6 4 2

Copyright © Mike Lupica, 2008
All rights reserved

THE LIBRARY OF CONGRESS HAS CATALOGED THE PHILOMEL BOOKS EDITION AS FOLLOWS:
Lupica, Mike. Long shot / Mike Lupica. p. cm. "A Comeback Kids novel."
Summary: Pedro, an avid basketball player, decides to run for class president,
challenging a teammate who is also one of the most popular boys in school.
ISBN: 978-0-399-24717-0(hc)
[1. Competition (Psychology)—Fiction. 2. Basketball—Fiction.
3. Self-confidence—Fiction. 4. Schools—Fiction.
5. Mexican Americans—Fiction.] I. Title.
PZ7.L97914Lo 2008 [Fic]—dc22 2008001385

Text set in Bookman

Puffin Books ISBN 978-0-14-241520-7

Printed in the United States of America

Once more for Taylor and our four children: Christopher, Alex, Zach and Hannah. They make me look for the best in these stories, the best in sports, the best in myself.

ACKNOWLEDGMENT

For my friend Luis Alberto Lopez, from Quetzaltenango, Guatemala. His restaurant is known as Chef Luis. His spirit infuses the pages of this book.

LONG SHOT

ONE

Pedro Morales loved playing basketball with Ned Hancock.

It didn't make Pedro different from any other sixth-grade basketball player at Vernon Middle School. Or in the whole town of Vernon for that matter. Ned made everybody around him better, every time he stepped on a court, whether it was for a real game or just scrimmaging.

But the thing Pedro liked best about playing with Ned is that Ned made *him* better.

Made him want to keep getting better at basketball.

And that meant every time Pedro stepped on a court.

Ned was doing that for him now, in the pickup game they were playing in the gym at the middle school. Which in their town, because the school district was so big, was for sixth-graders only. A school all their own is the way they looked at it, no seventh- or eighth-graders to bother them or bully them or bigtime them.

Today the kids had the gym all to themselves, school having been dismissed early because of teacher conferences. But Mr. Lucchino, the principal, had offered to stick around and let them use the gym, knowing that the first practice for the town team was the following Wednesday night, now that the players had been selected.

"Last day of spring training," Mr. Lucchino had said before rolling out the cart with the balls on it.

Pedro, a point guard, was on Ned's team today. Ned had picked him first even though he could have gone for a bigger guy. Ned liked playing with Pedro, too, because Pedro could pass. Not as well as Ned could. Nobody their age in Vernon could do anything in basketball as well as Ned could.

But Ned always wanted guys around him who knew how to pass. Even though he was only eleven years old, it was as if he already knew exactly how basketball was meant to be played. And that started with moving the ball.

Pedro felt the same way. Playing with Ned, going back to last year when they were old enough to play on their first town team together, reminded him why he loved basketball so much, loved it the way his father, who had been a star soccer player as a boy in Mexico, had always wanted him to love soccer.

Now the game Pedro and the rest of his friends were playing—first to ten baskets, didn't have to win by two—was tied at 9–all. Pedro's team had the ball. As they were taking it out under their basket, Ned said to Pedro, "Let's do this."

Ned was serious. It wasn't a pickup game to him now. If they were keeping score, he wanted to win. Even though they all knew there would be another game after this, and another game after that, until Mr. Lucchino finally told them to go wait out front for their parents.

When it was game point, Ned Hancock always played like he was playing for the championship of something, even if it was just the next time down the court.

Ned was a small forward, even though he wasn't small. He was tall enough to play center and a good enough shooter to play shooting guard. If he wanted to play point guard, he would have been better at handling and distributing the ball than Pedro was.

But he played forward. Point forward—that's the way Pedro thought of him, like they had two point guards in the game at the same time when they were on the same team.

Ned was a point *everything*, really.

Mr. Everything, that's what he was in basketball, and in their school, where he was the best student among the boys. He was even about to get elected president of Vernon Middle.

Forget about president of Vernon Middle, it was as if Ned was the mayor of all the kids their age in Vernon.

Before Ned inbounded the ball, he bent down to tie his sneakers, just as a way of buying a little time. As he did, he said to Pedro, "Let's run a high pick-and-roll. You and me. Just without the roll."

"Could you try that again in plain English?" Pedro said.

Ned did.

Pedro smiled as he began dribbling up the court.

Joe Sutter, the best rebounder in their grade and Pedro's best bud, was also on their team. Pedro wasn't worried about Joe getting in the way, because even though Joe didn't say much, he also didn't miss much. Sometimes he had a way of reading Pedro's mind, in a basketball game, a soccer game, or even in a video game.

Jeff Harmon—Ned's best bud—was guarding Pedro.

"Watch out for a trick play," Jeff called out. "I saw them talking down there."

Pedro was past half-court now, holding up a fist, which everybody on both teams knew meant absolutely nothing.

"Very funny," Jeff said.

No, Pedro thought, *just plain fun.*

This was always the best of it for him, in any sport, when he could see a play inside his head and was about to make it happen.

As soon as he began dribbling to his right, Joe cleared out of there and ran to the other side of the court. Like he just knew it was going to be a two-man game now—Ned and Pedro—the same way it had been so many times last season on the fifth-grade town team.

As soon as Joe cleared out, Ned came running up to what the announcers on television liked to call the "foul line extended," and set a monster pick on Jeff Harmon, who had been sliding to his left as he guarded Pedro. Jeff may have been Ned's bud, but it didn't help him now on game point, because when he ran into Ned's pick, nobody having called it out, Pedro could actually hear the air come out of him like it was coming out of a balloon.

Jeff was still sure he knew what was coming.

"Pick-and-roll!" he said, gasping for breath. "I've got Ned."

He stayed home on Ned. Bobby Murray left Ned now and picked up Pedro. And they would have had the play covered if Ned had kept going toward the basket, the way you were supposed to on the kind of pick-and-roll play they had been using all game long.

Only Ned, instead of cutting toward the basket, popped out a couple of steps *away* from it.

And instead of trying to beat Bobby Murray off the dribble, Pedro suddenly pulled up, too, spun and put the ball over his head and whipped a two-hand pass, hard, over to Ned.

The ball barely seemed to touch Ned's hands before it changed direction and came right back at Pedro.

Like the ball was on a string.

Or had bounced back to Pedro off some kind of invisible wall.

It was just enough to make Jeff Harmon turn his head. As soon as he did, Ned was gone.

The only thing missing was that *whoosh* you got in a superhero movie when Spidey or the Silver Surfer or one of those guys was there and gone.

Pedro didn't even bother catching the ball, just tap-passed it back to Ned over Jeff's head and over the rest of the defense, a sweet little floater of a pass, almost like they were playing volleyball on the beach and he was setting Ned up for a spike.

Ned didn't spike it. He just caught the ball and laid it up in one motion.

Ballgame.

Even a couple of the guys on defense put their hands together.

So did Mr. Lucchino, standing in the open gym door.

Pedro stood in the exact same spot from where he'd delivered the pass and watched as Ned, as usual, got high-fives all around. Joe once said that you didn't need one of those GPS guidance gizmos from your parents' car to locate Ned Hancock—just the sound of applause.

Everybody was acting as if Ned had somehow passed the ball to himself.

Pedro didn't care. If you played with Ned you knew it was his game, and you were just playing in it. It had pretty much been that way since they'd first become teammates, and Pedro accepted it. He was a point guard and he always remembered something he'd read once from a famous coach named Larry Brown, who said that the only stat that mattered for a point guard was the final score—whether or not his team had won the game, not how many points and assists he had.

Their team had won, and that was enough for Pedro. That and the satisfaction of making that pass, delivering that baby like it was the afternoon mail.

He quietly walked over to the water fountain to get himself a drink before they started up all over again.

Joe Sutter, when he did talk, liked to say that the best thing about his buddy Pedro was that he knew who he was. He never needed to be a star, on any team he'd ever played for. He didn't need to put himself out there, to say to everybody, *Hey, look at me.*

He just wanted to win the game.

TWO

Even though it was November and soccer season had just ended for Pedro's town team, it hadn't ended for him and his dad.

For the two of them, on Saturday mornings at least, soccer season didn't end until there was snow on the ground.

For Pedro, the best part of soccer Saturdays wasn't running around on his school's soccer field, it was being with his dad. Because more than any professional athlete, Luis Morales was Pedro's hero.

They were on the field at Vernon Middle even earlier than usual because Luis had to work later that day. The way he had been working every day lately, getting ready to open his own restaurant in Vernon's downtown district.

The restaurant was going to be called Casa Luis, and Pedro knew it was so much more than a restaurant to his dad. It was the dream he had carried in his head from the time he had come across the border from Mexico—legally, he always pointed out to Pedro—with his own parents as a teenager.

He had lived in Tucson, Arizona, first and then moved to New York City, because that had been another dream of his when he envisioned a better life for himself in America.

Once he got to New York he worked as a bus-boy as a way of putting himself through cooking school. Then he had worked his way up to being a chef, finally becoming head chef at Miller's, the best restaurant in Vernon, where Pedro was born and had lived his whole life.

Earlier this year, Luis Morales had found a space he could afford, after saving up for a long time, and now he was about to open Casa Luis. He'd been working so hard at it, day and night, wanting everything to be just right and look just right, that Pedro hadn't been seeing very much of him lately.

Pedro had even told his dad at breakfast this morning that he could skip soccer today if he was too busy at the restaurant.

His father looked across the table at him with eyes as dark as Pedro's, but which seemed to see so much more, as always.

"Boy," he said, "I would sooner give up eating one of my own desserts before I would give up my soccer mornings with you."

Luis Morales had been the best player in his town in Mexico as a boy. And one of his boyhood dreams had been to play for Mexico in the World Cup when he got older.

"But that is the funny thing about dreams," Pedro's dad liked to say. "Just when you are sure you have a good one, an even better one comes along."

By the time he had left Mexico at the age of fifteen, he'd also left behind whatever big ideas he had about being a World Cup soccer star. Now soccer was a passion more than a dream, but a passion that Luis always made time for. He watched games from all over the world thanks to satellite television, and even played in what he called an "old man's league" in Camden, the next town over from Vernon, in the fall and spring.

Pedro had watched his dad play some of those old man games, watched him and thought that *his* old man was the most dazzling one out there, running rings around the other players, almost playing a different game than anybody else.

And even with all that, Pedro never thought he was seeing the very best of Luis Morales.

It was as if his dad saved that for Pedro and their Saturday mornings together.

What Pedro really saw from his dad, what he was seeing again today as they passed the ball to each other and tried to take it away from each other or took turns in goal, was this:

The boy in Mexico who was going to play in the World Cup someday.

Pedro felt like he'd traveled back in time so he and his dad could be the same age for a little while.

Pedro was quick. His dad, even now, was quicker. Pedro, whose normal position in soccer was midfielder, could do a lot with the ball.

His dad could always do more.

Luis Morales even had this trick—it really seemed like a magic trick to Pedro—where he would lean forward and balance a ball between his shoulder blades and remove the T-shirt he was wearing without the ball falling to the ground.

He did that now on the soccer field at Vernon Middle when they took a break.

"It's like something I saw on a television show once, Papa," Pedro said. "A man pulled a table-cloth off a table, but the glasses and silverware and plates stayed where they were."

His dad smiled.

Another thing that made him look young, like a boy, to Pedro.

"Anybody can do *that*," his dad said. "But only your papa can do what I do with this soccer ball."

"I believe you," Pedro said, smiling back at him.

It was all right for his dad to take his shirt off because the November sun was warm this morning. They were both on their backs now, using their soccer balls as headrests, both taking the sun full on their faces.

Luis Morales said, "Are you absolutely sure of this thing you tell me, that you love basketball more than soccer?"

Pedro said, "It's not that I don't love soccer. I just love basketball more."

"How could such a thing happen?" his dad said. Pedro turned his head slightly and saw that his father was still smiling, his face as bright as the morning.

"It just happened," Pedro said. "I couldn't help it."

"Ahhh," his dad said. "It's like a prettier girl has come along to steal your heart." He sighed and said, "So the Americanization of my boy is complete."

"You always tell me that you can be anything you want to be in America," Pedro said. "Well, I've decided I want to be a great basketball player."

His father sat up now. "Then you must work at it, my boy," he said.

"You know I work, Papa," Pedro said. "Not

as hard as you. Nobody works as hard as you. But I work at sports and I work at school. I want to make you and Mom proud of me."

His mother, Anne, had been born in Vernon, had spent her whole life there except for college, and now worked a few days a week at the best clothing store in town, True Blue. She wasn't Mexican-American, just what Pedro thought of as American-American, with blond hair and blue eyes.

"It is a fine thing, wanting to make your parents proud," Luis Morales said. "But it is much more important to make yourself proud."

It was another thing that Pedro loved about Saturday mornings. It was as if he and his father saved their best talking for the soccer field.

Pedro sat up now, because he wanted to make sure his dad knew that he had his full attention, like this was his favorite class and Luis Morales was his favorite teacher in the world.

"I don't just want you to look for the best in sports," Pedro's dad said. "I want you to look for the best in your*self*."

"I will," Pedro said. "You know I will."

"The more you love something," his dad said, "the harder you work at it. And then, if you are lucky, you finally learn the secret that I remember every time I walk through the door to what will soon be my restaurant."

"What secret?" Pedro said.

"That being there isn't work at all."

Pedro could see how excited his father was, saying these things, and it made him excited, too, made him feel as if the morning sunshine had somehow gotten even brighter.

"If you have the talent and you have the will, then nothing is out of your reach," his dad said. "When I was working as a busboy in New York City, some of the other busboys would laugh when I told them I would have my own restaurant someday. Well, if they could see me now, they wouldn't be laughing."

He moved closer to Pedro and put his hands on his son's shoulders.

"I don't know if you have greatness in you as a basketball player," his dad said. "That is between you and basketball, because sports sorts these things out eventually, tells us all whether we are good enough to be great or not. But no-body can stop you from being a leader, my son. Just watching you on the field, I see already that you are a leader. I wish your mother and I could take credit for that, but it's something I believe in my heart you must be born with."

"I just do my best," Pedro said.

"It is more than that," his dad said. "Even the other leaders on your teams follow you."

Pedro smiled. "You're prejudiced."

"No," Luis Morales said. "I just know a great leader when I see one. And you know what I say about great leaders, don't you?"

He did.

Pedro smiled again at his father, because he did know what he always said, because he knew what was coming next. He always knew, the way he knew the soccer ball would stay between his dad's shoulder blades when his shirt came off, every single time.

"In this country," Luis Morales said, "great leaders can grow up to be president."

"I know, Papa."

"I don't want you to just know," his dad said. "I want you to believe."

Then his dad was pulling him up, wrapping him in a bear hug, putting his face close to Pedro's, Pedro feeling the scratch of his beard, his dad's face rough even though he had just shaved. Pedro felt the way he always did when his dad put his arms around him: good and happy and safe.

"President Morales," his dad said now.

Pedro laughed.

"Do you believe?"

"Papa . . . "

"I want to know you believe. Let me hear you say it and I will do the bicycle kick for you."

"Fine, I'll say it. President Pedro Morales."

"No, say it like you believe."

"President Pedro Morales!" Pedro said, louder this time, grinning all the while.

"That's what I want to hear!" his father said, then stood up.

Luis Morales wasn't big, even though he had always seemed big to Pedro. He seemed bigger than ever now, standing there between Pedro and the blue sky.

Pedro watched as his dad's feet started playing with the soccer ball as if they had a mind of their own, left foot first then right, the ball bouncing off a knee, then off his dad's head, then back to his feet without touching the ground.

Now Luis Morales turned his back to the goal they had been using, and Pedro knew he was ready for the bicycle kick.

Pelé's kick.

First the left knee came up. Then his right leg, his kicking leg, was coming up, Luis Morales really looking as if he were pedaling a bike backward. Then the left leg came down as the right leg was kicking through the ball, looking as if it were one of those perfect right angles they studied in geometry.

It always looked as if his dad, as graceful as he was, was somehow going to kick himself in the head.

Only he never did.

He just buried the ball in the back of the net.

"See," he said. "You work hard enough at

something, and *anything* is possible. Isn't that right, Mr. President?"

"Yes, Papa," Pedro said.

They went home after that, and Pedro's dad went off to his restaurant, getting it ready for its grand opening in about a month. Pedro had told Joe he would call him when he got back from the soccer field and they would hang out later.

But first he went up to his room, the one with the Fathead poster, like a 3-D image, of Steve Nash on his wall, the one that made it seem as if Nash was about to make a bounce pass with the ball in his right hand right across Pedro's bedroom.

Only Pedro wasn't thinking about basketball right now.

Or about soccer.

He was thinking about his dad.

He had heard his speech about a hundred times before, or maybe a thousand. But today it was as if he had heard it for the first time, as if his dad's words hadn't just gotten into his head this time, but all the way into his heart.

Pedro's English teacher, Mr. Randolph, liked

to talk about what he called the "blink moment," which was his way of describing the idea from which great stories and great books came—a great idea being born in the blink of an eye.

Mr. Randolph said that no one ever knew when a blink moment happened. They just happened.

And Pedro knew one had happened to him on that soccer field this morning.

President Morales.

THREE

Pedro had two private places he liked best, places where he was completely happy to be alone with a basketball, places where he did his best thinking.

One was the full outdoor court at Carinor Park. The other was the miniature court his dad had built for him next to their garage. It wasn't the size of a real half-court, but it was big enough to shoot from the corner and shoot free throws and then move back beyond the partial three-point line Pedro had drawn on the smooth cement Luis Morales had lovingly laid down himself.

This is where Pedro found himself now, working on his outside shot.

Pedro Morales was constantly working on his

shooting, simply because it was the weakest part of his game.

By a lot.

He could make free throws just fine, especially when he had to. And he had made the occasional outside shot. Just not as many as he wanted to make, not as many as he knew he'd *have* to make someday to be the complete player he wanted to be.

He had always played the game with a pass-first mentality, from the time he began playing organized ball at the Vernon YMCA, and it wasn't just because he thought of himself as a playmaker, doing what good playmakers and great point guards were supposed to do. That was just one reason. The bigger reason, and he knew it better than anybody, was that he just didn't have the same confidence shooting the ball that he did passing it.

If he saw an opening on the court, he knew he could make the pass.

When he was open for a fifteen- or twenty-footer, he only *hoped* he could make the shot.

Huge difference.

He was a better passer than scorer in soccer, as well, but even in soccer he knew that if he had the open shot, he was taking it, and burying the sucker. Money, every time.

He wanted in the worst way to be money shooting a basketball.

Neither Steve Nash nor Chris Paul was the best outside shooter in the world, but if you left them alone, they could both burn you from beyond the three-point arc, and that threat made them even better at playmaking.

Pedro wanted to be *that* kind of point guard.

He had been watching a show on ESPN Classic the other day, about Magic Johnson, and they were talking about how even though the Lakers had won the championship his rookie year and he was MVP of the NBA Finals, he knew he had to improve his outside shot if he wanted to be the kind of complete player he needed to be. So he went home to Michigan that summer and shot about a thousand outside shots and when he came back for his second season, he started making bombs if you left him alone, and made the whole league come out and guard him.

"Even though we won the title," Magic said, "I knew I had work to do."

Pedro had never been afraid of hard work. So he showed up early for practice and stayed late sometimes to work on his shot, and on weekends he even worked harder.

So after soccer today, after his dad had gone to work at the restaurant, he went outside to the end of their driveway and shot for two hours, shot so much that he had to rest at times because he was too tired to raise his arms over his head.

And today he was making them.

Usually one of his problems was that he thought too much about his shot, worried too much about his form and his technique, instead of just looking at the basket and letting it go, like they told you to do in all the shooting books.

Sometimes Pedro thought it wasn't just that he was thinking too much, it was that he *wanted* it too much.

Not today.

Today he was on fire, and maybe it was because he was thinking about wanting something else: to be class president. Today he couldn't get his mind off that, couldn't get the idea out of his head now that it was rattling around in there like one of his line-drive shots.

The less Pedro thought about shooting from the outside today, the better he did.

For this one day, at least, the long shot was actually making some.

He didn't say anything to his parents about wanting to run for president. Didn't say anything to Joe Sutter when they went to the movies on Sunday.

Mostly, Pedro kept waiting for the idea to get out of his head.

Only it wouldn't.

Even though the voice inside his head kept reminding him of one crucial point: Running for president of the school meant running against Ned Hancock.

Who never lost at anything.

He finally told Joe at lunch on Monday.

"Tell me I'm nuts," Pedro said.

"No can do."

"You don't think running against Ned is nuts?"

"Nope."

"Then *you're* nuts," Pedro said.

"Should have thought of this myself," Joe said. "You ought to be president of this school, even if it does mean going up against Ned."

"Right," Pedro said. "Piece of cake. He's the best athlete our age, he's the most popular kid in class. And, oh, by the way? He's probably better in school than he is at football or basketball or baseball."

Joe said, "Dude, you must be trying to talk yourself out of this, because you're not talking me out of it."

"I'm just saying."

"And *I'm* just saying," Joe said. "You're smarter than he is, and not just about school stuff. And guess what else? He probably doesn't even care about being class president, he just thinks it's one more thing he's *supposed* to be.

One more honor that's supposed to be his. Like being captain of every team he plays on."

"Because he is supposed to be!" Pedro said.

"Why are you shouting?" Joe said, grinning at him.

"I'm not shouting!"

"Could've fooled me."

"The more I talk about this, the more I think the one who'd be fooling himself would be *me*," Pedro said.

"Ned Hancock only *thinks* he's the coolest kid in our class," Joe said. "You actually are. Even though I can't believe I'm actually saying that to you."

"You sure are chatty all of a sudden."

"This is a great idea, even if it wasn't mine," Joe said.

"It sounded a lot better when I was the one thinking it," Pedro said. "Now I'm afraid that if I say it to anybody else, they're going to fall down laughing."

"Not Sarah," Joe said. "Not Bobby. Not Jamal."

Sarah Layng and Bobby Murray and Jamal Wynne, the center on the basketball team, were the other members of their crew. Usually they all ate lunch together, but today Sarah and Bobby and Jamal were part of a community-service group, serving lunch at the Vernon Home for the Aged.

"Sarah ought to be the one running against Ned, not me."

"Dude, you can't unthink this," Joe said. "You are so doing this."

Just then the bell sounded, followed by a burst of laughter from the other side of the room. Pedro looked over to see Ned Hancock with the same crew he always had around him. Ned was a head taller than everybody else, almost like he was up in a different atmosphere, always above the crowd.

"C'mon, President Morales," Joe said, "time for English."

"Please don't call me that," Pedro said. "Especially around normal people."

"Got a nice ring to it, though, doesn't it?" Joe said.

Pedro wasn't going to admit it to his best bud—he didn't want to encourage him. But one thing hadn't changed since Saturday morning:

It *did* have a nice ring to it.

More than anything, more than being a good player or a good teammate or even being the leader that his dad said he was, Pedro Morales thought of himself as being honest.

Prided himself on being honest.

That was his big thing. He was honest about what his strengths and weaknesses were, in school and in sports, with his classmates in the sixth grade and with his teammates on whatever team he was playing on at the time. It was another one of Luis Morales's big speeches, his dad telling him constantly that if you told the truth in everything you did, then you had nothing to worry about.

"The truth is the easiest thing to remember," Luis Morales said. "Lies? They're harder to remember than the hardest homework assignment in the world."

Pedro was trying to be honest with himself

about running for president. He knew how much he wanted to do it, despite what he had said to Joe. He knew he wanted to prove to himself, in his own life, what his dad had always said about being able to do anything you wanted in this world if you set your mind to it.

But, because he was honest, he knew what kind of a long shot he would be against somebody like Ned Hancock, who every kid in school seemed to know already, even if they hadn't grown up with him.

And yet, despite everything Pedro had said to Joe at lunch, how crazy it all sounded when you said you were running for president, when the words were in the air around you, Pedro could only hear one voice inside his head the rest of the afternoon: his dad's.

He kept thinking that if his dad could finally open his restaurant, then anything really was possible, because who was more of a long shot than Luis Morales, the poor kid from Mexico?

By the time they were in the bus line at three o'clock, almost like he was reading Pedro's mind, Joe brought it up again.

"C'mon, dude," he said. "Let's do this."

Pedro gave him a nervous smile. "Maybe," he said.

Joe Sutter, who sometimes seemed to be half-asleep even when he was wide-awake, immediately said, *"Yes!"* Then he put his right arm out and pulled it back like he was pulling a lever.

Like one of those voting-booth levers they'd seen on the real Election Day in their town, on a class trip just last week.

"I said *maybe,*" Pedro said.

"Might be what you *said,*" Joe said. "But that's not what I heard, Mr. President."

Then he nodded as the bus line started to move and said, "This is going to be epic."

Probably an epic disaster, Pedro thought.

But his mind was made up.

FOUR

For Pedro, Wednesday was going to be a big day, just because the first official practice for the Vernon town team was scheduled for six o'clock, in one of the gyms at the high school. But now it would be even bigger, because at the end of the school day an assembly was being held at which the nominations for class president would be made.

"Tell me again I'm doing the right thing," Pedro said to Joe on the bus on the way to school.

"No."

"*No?*"

"You already know it's the right thing or you wouldn't have thought about it in the first place and you wouldn't be doing it," Joe said.

So far Joe was the only one who knew Pedro *was* doing it, because Pedro still hadn't told the others in his crew.

In the bus now Pedro said to Joe, "What do you think Sarah and the guys are going to say?"

"What I'm saying," Joe said. "Just do it."

Pedro grinned. "I think you stole that from somebody."

When Pedro did tell Sarah and Bobby and Jamal at lunch, Sarah immediately punched Pedro in the arm—hard—and said, "No *way*."

"Okay, I'm not rubbing my arm. It wouldn't be the guy thing to do," Pedro said. "But that hurt."

Bobby Murray just reached across the lunch table, pounded Pedro some fist, then decided to put his hand up for a high-five too.

"Can't believe you're gonna go one-on-one with the fresh prince of the school," Jamal said.

The Fresh Prince of Bel-Air was Jamal's favorite TV show on Nickelodeon, Will Smith being his all-time hero.

"Does Ned know yet?" Sarah said.

"Nah," Pedro said, looking across the room

to where Ned was sitting with his friends. "What am I supposed to do, walk over and say, 'Hope you don't mind, I'm planning to take five or six votes away from you.'"

Joe pointed a finger at Pedro and said to the rest of them, "See how confident he is?"

Pedro said, "Just keeping it real. Isn't that what you're always telling me?"

"I want to be campaign manager," Bobby said. "Or does that require actual work?"

Across the room there was one of those huge laughs that always seemed to be coming from Ned's table.

"See, he's laughing already," Pedro said. "Maybe he does know."

"There's that no-worries attitude again," Joe said.

"I want to be the one to second the nomination after Joe makes it," Sarah said.

"How come you get to second?" Jamal said.

"I'm gonna help him bring in the girl vote, that's why," Sarah said.

To Pedro she said, "I'll be your campaign manager, too."

"Okay," Pedro said. It was never a good idea to mess with Sarah, on anything.

"Have you ever said no to her?" Joe said.

Sarah smiled. "The candidate is under no obligation to answer that question."

Sarah acted older than the rest of them. She also thought older, talked older, probably *was* secretly older, Pedro had always thought.

After that, it was their table doing most of the laughing in the cafeteria, Pedro's friends demanding a three-day school week, four free periods per day, and a month off for Christmas, at least.

One night of homework a week.

Tops.

"Just remember one thing," Jamal said. "If we're in it, we win it."

"True that," Bobby Murray said.

"In it to win it," Jamal said again.

"I wish," Pedro said.

"Okay, that's it," Joe said. "We gotta get your first campaign promise right now."

Pedro looked at him, knowing just from his tone of voice that he meant business.

"No more talk, even fooling-around talk, about losing from now on," he said to Pedro. "Deal?"

Pedro made a face now like he was about to take medicine.

"I don't know . . . "

"Deal or no deal?" Joe said, like the guy on the television show.

"Deal," Pedro said finally.

He put his hand out to the middle of the table, and they all put theirs on top of his.

In it to win it.

FIVE

They held the assembly in the school auditorium. All three hundred kids who had come from the four elementary schools in the Vernon school district squeezed in there, filling the rows of folding chairs that stretched back from the stage.

To Pedro, the place sounded louder than the arena where his dad had taken him last year to watch Steve Nash and the Suns play the Nets—the first time he had seen his favorite point guard play in person.

Mr. Lucchino finally went up on stage to the microphone and quieted everybody down. He reminded them that this was an assembly and not recess, and officially welcomed them to what he called "this year's nominating convention." He instructed them that class elections were something taken quite seriously at Vernon Middle School, not just by the administration, but by past students as well.

"You can look around you today and see how big our school really is," Mr. Lucchino said. Then he shook his head and said, "And how loud," and that got a laugh out of the kids in the auditorium.

Pedro could feel the heavy beat of his heart now, felt it even more than he had when he and Joe and Sarah and the rest of their guys had first taken their seats in a row of chairs about halfway back from the stage.

"And I want you to know that being class president at our school is not some honorary position," he said. "The person who wins this election will help me run what we call town meetings about various school issues, will join the Honor Council, which makes sure the laws of our school are obeyed, and will give the keynote speech at graduation this year."

Mr. Lucchino paused then, looked out at the audience, and said, "This isn't just a popularity contest. This is about being a leader."

The principal of Pedro's school was sounding exactly like his dad now.

Pedro half expected Mr. Lucchino to keep going and start talking about America.

Once more, he heard his father's voice inside his head.

President Morales.

If Papa only knew, Pedro thought.

It was quiet for a moment, because Mr. Lucchino was still at the podium. Pedro had Sarah on his left and Joe on his right. He wondered if either one of them could hear his heart now, pounding away like there was an entire drum set inside him.

Then Mr. Lucchino explained the process. Candidates would be nominated and seconded, and then the nominee would announce from the stage who his vice president would be.

The highlight of the campaign would be the day when the candidates for president had a debate in front of the school, and then gave their speeches.

Sarah whispered into Pedro's ear. "The campaign hasn't even started and I am *so* into it."

"Not nearly as into it as you're going to be," Pedro said.

"What does that mean?" she said.

Pedro just smiled and put a finger to his lips. Sarah's response was to jab him with one of her elbows.

"So," Mr. Lucchino said, "without further ado, we will accept the first nomination for president of Vernon Middle School."

Pedro couldn't catch his breath now, feeling as if he'd just finished running wind sprints.

"Showtime," Jamal said from down the row.

Pedro could have sworn Mr. Lucchino was looking right at Ned Hancock as he said, "Okay, who'd like to go first?"

Jeff Harmon and Dave DeLuca were sitting in the front row, on either side of Ned. They ran toward the stage now as if it were a race to see which one of them could get to the microphone first.

In the crowd, a lot of the other kids were already applauding, almost by force of habit.

Jeff started it off, playing up his big moment, saying in a deep announcer's voice, "I would like to place in nomination of the name of the next . . . "

When he paused there, Joe said to Pedro, "The next American Idol?"

" . . . president of the sixth grade . . . *Ned Hancock*!"

Over the cheers that erupted in the auditorium now, Bobby yelled into the microphone, "Second!"

More cheers, like Ned had just won another big game for one of his teams.

Then Ned walked up, taking his time, smiling, not sweating this because he never seemed to sweat anything. He walked across the stage as if he owned it, owned the whole place, really. He calmly stepped to the microphone and said, "I accept."

More cheers.

Then he said, "And I pick Jeff Harmon to be vice president."

Another cheer.

Ned not saying he was picking Jeff to run with him, Pedro noted. Picking him to *be* vice president.

Like they'd won the election already, without a vote. Won by "acclamation"—something Pedro had just learned in Social Studies when they'd begun talking in class about the upcoming school election, before he'd even thought about running.

When everybody quieted down, Mr. Lucchino said, "Anybody else?"

Nobody moved.

The principal looked one way, then the other.

"Is Mr. Hancock really going to run unopposed?" he said.

Still nothing.

Pedro began to wonder if Joe had changed his mind.

"Anybody at all?" Mr. Lucchino said. "Because if not, I'd actually be forced to select somebody myself . . . "

Joe stood up then, as if he'd been waiting for just the right moment, maybe wanting Ned to think that he *was* running unopposed.

Joe made his way down their aisle, slowly walking toward the stage as if he was the one who had all day now. He made his way even more slowly across the stage to the podium.

When he got there, he looked over the crowd, still no expression on his face, leaned in and said, "Pedro Morales."

Sarah stood up, shot her hand straight up into the air the way she did in class when she had the right answer, and shouted out, "I second the nomination of Pedro Morales!"

No applause this time.

The only sound in the auditorium was the rustling of clothes as some of the kids in the front rows turned around to look at Pedro.

Bobby started to put his hands together until Pedro stopped him, not wanting some sort of pity clap from one of his friends.

Then Pedro went toward the stage, trying to make sure he wasn't running, even though he wanted this over as soon as possible. He knew enough about himself to know this as he made his way up the steps: The guy who'd never wanted to draw attention to himself, who just wanted to be a *team* guy, was certainly the center of attention now.

He got to the podium and said, "I accept."

No reaction to that either. But then he heard Mr. Lucchino behind him, saying, "Pedro, you've got to speak into the microphone."

This time he leaned forward, but as he did, the mike poked him right in the nose.

That got a reaction.

Laughter from the audience.

Pedro went back in again, feeling how red his face must have looked, and said, "I accept," then raced right into the next part, saying, "And I choose Sarah Layng to run with me."

He wasn't even sure how much they heard after Sarah's name because he was pulling back from the mike, wanting to get off the stage as soon as possible.

Mr. Lucchino came back to the microphone for the last time now, to give them the official dates for the candidates' speeches next week. He told the candidates that they were allowed to make posters for themselves, or have posters made. Then he said the assembly was dismissed.

When Pedro got back to his row, Sarah was standing, hands on hips, but she was smiling.

He turned and pointed to his arm and said, "Why don't we just skip right to the part where you slug me again for keeping the vice president thing a secret."

"Why don't I hug you instead?" she said.

"Not a chance," Pedro said.

Pedro told his crew that he'd catch up with them, that there was something he had to do.

"What?" Joe said.

"I gotta say something to Ned."

"I'll wait with you," Joe said.

Pedro wasn't sure exactly what he wanted to say to him, just feeling as if he needed to say something before they were together at basketball practice later.

Ned came walking down the center aisle, Jeff on one side of him, Dave on the other.

Joe stood with Pedro.

When Ned got close enough, Pedro smiled and put out his hand. And for a moment, Pedro thought Ned was going to leave him hanging. He looked down at Pedro's hand.

Finally he slapped him a casual low five, not much on it. They'd always been closer as teammates than as friends, but had always gotten along fine with each other away from the court.

"Good luck," Pedro said. "Not that you're going to need it."

"Didn't know you were running, dude," Ned said.

"Tell you the truth," Pedro said, "neither did I."

"Hey, I've got a question," Jeff Harmon said in a loud voice, because it was the only kind of voice he had, as if he went through life with his very own bullhorn. "Why *are* you running, Pete?"

He was the only kid in school who called him that, and Pedro never really understood why, except it seemed to be a way for Jeff Harmon to put him down. Like he could do that by Americanizing Pedro's name, even though Pedro had been born in Vernon the same as Jeff had, the same as all his friends. He'd never thought he was different just because of his last name, or because his dad had been born in another country.

This time he decided not to let it go.

"It's *Pedro*," he said.

Jeff ignored him, turned to Ned and Bobby and said in a loud voice, "Guess *Pedro* here never heard of a little thing called a landslide."

In a quiet voice, Joe said, "Wow. Landslide. Learn a new word today, Harmon?"

"Hey guys, chill," Ned said now. "We're all teammates, remember?"

It was true, all five of them were on the town team, and sometimes they were the five on the court.

"Ned's right," Pedro said.

"And teammates are supposed to stick, right?" Ned said.

Then before Pedro or anybody else could agree with him on that, Ned Hancock said, "Even when they decide to run against each other."

Now he looked right at Pedro as if he were looking at him for the first time, as if he'd turned into a stranger.

"Right, Pete?" he said, grinning.

And in that moment, it was as if Ned was the one who had turned into a stranger.

Then Ned and his buds were out the double doors and gone.

SIX

The gym at Vernon High School was so big they could pull down a divider from the ceiling and make it two separate gyms on weekends once the town teams started playing games.

Tonight the sixth-grade team, the Vernon Knights, was at the high school. And just out of sheer luck, they didn't have to share the gym with anybody.

"Madison Square Vernon," Joe said when they walked in.

As far as Pedro was concerned, having the whole gym to themselves just made the night better. The newly polished floor, the overhead lights brighter than ever, everything feeling clean, as if you could just feel the whole season stretching out in all directions.

Even after the way the assembly had ended, with Pedro feeling as if he'd been called out— weirded out, really—by Ned and his friends, he was still excited, in an almost goofy, Christmas-morning way, to have the basketball season start, right here and right now.

It seemed to Pedro that everybody had shown up tonight with new sneakers—Jamal called them "right-out-the-box kicks"—and just the sound of them, the crazy, constant squeak of them on the polished floor, was like the best possible music downloaded straight to Pedro's ears.

Their coach, Cory Harwell, was the same one they'd had from fifth-grade town ball, a coach they all loved playing for and couldn't believe had moved up along with them. Coach Cory—as they all called him—had played Division I college ball for Vermont, even though he was only five-seven and looked enough like the little guard the Knicks had, Nate Robinson, to be his twin brother.

Coach Cory didn't just look like a kid, he acted as happy as one, happy as any of them, to be back on this court.

If they weren't pumped already, the sound of his voice—a voice that was a whole lot bigger than Coach Cory was—was really pumping up the volume now, echoing all over the big gym, bouncing off the walls and the ceiling as he got them right into a three-man weave fast-break drill.

"Pass and cut behind!" he was yelling from the half-court line. "Pass and cut behind. Uh-*huh*. Move that ball and move yourselves. Uh-*huh*." Turning basketball into rap, getting them right into it in the first ten minutes of practice.

A few minutes later Pedro ended up in the middle, Ned in the right lane, Jeff Harmon to Pedro's left. Pedro didn't need any help from Coach Cory to get into this particular drill—it was one of his favorites, even though a lot of the guys thought it was boring. He loved making crisp passes, running at full speed, making his cuts behind the other two guys as tight as possible, like he was rounding a base in baseball. Loved seeing if the three guys in his group could make good enough passes and cuts that they could get in more than the five passes Coach

Cory wanted them to throw before somebody got a layup without the ball once touching the floor.

"Make every one a thing of beauty!" Coach Cory yelled now. "Like my own dream girl Beyoncé!"

The last pass was supposed to go to Ned, and Pedro thought he'd led him perfectly. But for some reason Ned slowed up just enough, maybe just to get his footwork right for the layup, and Pedro's pass wound up too far in front of him. The ball kept going all the way through an open door and out of the gym.

Making it look like a worse pass than it really was.

Pedro smacked his hands together hard, in frustration, the sound like a firecracker going off in the gym.

"What's the matter, Morales?" Coach Cory said. He was smiling, but he usually smiled when he was getting his message across. "Forget how to make a simple chest pass over the summer?"

Now Pedro just put his head down, embarrassed. He knew Coach was playing with him a little, knew it was just their first practice, knew it was a drill he hardly ever messed up. But Pedro didn't know anybody who liked being called out by the coach this way, even in fun.

"Okay," Coach Cory said, "now I gotta put the pressure on everybody, right from the jump. We're gonna run this baby ten times perfect, or I'm gonna make you suckers run ten laps for me."

It was, Pedro knew by now, Coach Cory's way. He made basketball fun. Just never easy. Made you laugh a lot. But made you learn more. He wanted you to do even the littlest things right, said it was like building a team from the foundation up, and then from there, once you had the strong foundation, it was just second nature for you to play the game right.

And, boy, did he not want to tell you the same thing twice.

After playing a whole season with Coach Cory already, Pedro looked at it this way: Coach wanted you to *play* basketball, but made you work at the same time.

Fine with Pedro.

He'd never been afraid of hard work.

They all got through the weave nine straight times. Now Pedro was back in the middle for the last one before they got to scrimmage. Ned was on his left this time, Joe on his right.

Pass, cut behind.

Simple.

Do it again and keep doing it until the last layup, the one that meant they could break up into teams and *really* play some ball.

The three of them had done the drill so well, so cleanly, that they'd already passed it five times by the time Ned hooked around from the left and Pedro was flying from the right for his layup. Cake. Ned was a dream passer of the ball, whether it was a long pass or a short one, chest or bounce. He'd throw it hard to you but never too hard, always giving you a pass you could not only handle, but *do* something with, pass it or shoot it or just put it on the floor and start dribbling.

Not this time.

The ball came at Pedro harder than he expected, harder than he ever got from Ned, and just low enough that before Pedro could get his hands down, his knee caught the ball just right and sent it screaming so hard off the back wall that it was as if Pedro had booted it there.

"Soccer season's over," Coach Cory yelled. "You gotta *catch* that ball, my brother." He blew his whistle then. "So now we run," he said.

"How many laps, Coach?" Bobby Murray said, maybe hoping he'd forgotten.

"Ten."

Groans all around.

As they ran, Pedro heard a voice behind him whisper, "Nice going, Pete."

He thought it might be Ned. Or maybe it was Jeff. He couldn't be sure. It was one of them, though. Pedro knew that.

He just put his head down and ran harder, promising himself he'd made the last mistake he was going to make for the rest of the night.

Things didn't get any better when they scrimmaged. If anything they got worse, courtesy of Ned Hancock.

Sometimes Ned would wait a couple of extra seconds when Pedro was open, giving the guy covering him a chance to get back on him. Or he would give Pedro a look the way he always had, but then cut the wrong way, and Pedro would throw the ball away just like he had during the three-man weave.

One time, after Pedro did that and got called out by Coach Cory again, Ned came over and said, "Don't worry, dude, by next week we'll be reading each other's minds again."

Or maybe I'm reading yours loud and clear right now, Pedro thought.

During a quick water break near the end of practice, Pedro whispered to Joe, "Are you see-ing what's happening out there?"

Joe said, "Yeah. You're trying to do too much and it's messing you up big-time."

"You think it's all me?"

Joe grinned and looked back over his shoul-der, as if Pedro might be talking to somebody else. "No," Joe said. "The hoops fairy."

For the last ten minutes of the scrimmage, Coach Cory decided to mix up the teams, then told them they were going full court, and to forget about running plays, he just wanted them to *run*, to force the action, every chance they got.

"Pressure wins in this sport," he said. "The pressure you put on the other guy, and then the pressure they start putting on themselves."

When they started to match up, picking the guys they were going to guard, Ned Hancock raised a hand and said, "Coach, you mind if I play point on our side? I want to work on my ballhandling a little."

"Knock yourself out," Coach Cory said. "It's your team."

Pedro thought, *Yeah, in more ways than one tonight.*

"Thanks," he said, and then added, "I guess I've got Pedro."

They *never* guarded each other in practice, except if it was on a switch. For starters, Ned was at least a head taller than Pedro. And that wasn't even the biggest problem, which was Ned's length—those long arms of his that could swallow up even guys his own size when Ned really went after it on defense.

And, boy, did he ever go after it now.

He smothered Pedro every chance he got, guarded him all over the court, and stayed right up on him even when Pedro wasn't close to being in the play.

On the last play of the night, he put such a good ball fake on Pedro that he got his feet tangled up and fell down as Ned blew past him on the baseline for an easy layup.

When Coach Cory blew the whistle for the last time, Ned ran over, smiling, and put a hand out.

"For Pete's sake, dude," he said. "The fake wasn't *that* good, was it?"

Pedro ignored his hand and pulled himself to his feet.

Yeah, Pedro thought. *For Pete's sake.*

And in that moment he knew something as sure as he knew his screen name and his password: He didn't have to wait until school tomorrow for the campaign to begin.

It had already begun.

SEVEN

After practice, his mom dropped him off at Sarah's house, which was only three blocks away from theirs.

Pedro was going to eat dinner at Sarah's and then the two of them were going to study together for a history test they were having tomorrow.

That's what Pedro told his mom and that much was true, because Pedro didn't lie to his parents, ever. What he didn't tell his mom—or his dad—was that after they finished studying, they were going to make their first campaign posters, hoping to get the jump on Ned and Jeff.

Sarah made sure to tell her mom not to say anything to Pedro's mom, that he wanted to surprise his parents about running for president.

Pedro hadn't told his mom about being nominated when he got home from school, hadn't told her on the way to Sarah's, and frankly wasn't sure when he was going to tell anybody in his family.

"When are you going to let them in on our little secret?" Sarah said in her room. "I know this isn't the smallest town in the world, but somebody might mention it to your parents one of these days, right?"

"It's not that big a deal," Pedro said.

Sarah saw right through that one like a head fake she wasn't falling for.

"If it's not a big deal," she said, "then why are you treating it like one?"

"I just keep thinking about having to tell them that we lost," he said.

He remembered something he'd seen once on ESPN, famous athletes talking about how they motivated themselves to win a big game. This one tennis player, Chris Evert, said that she always imagined the same thing: the look on the other player's face at the net if she beat her.

Pedro was just turning that around now, but with his dad. Pedro just couldn't bear to think of the look on his dad's face when he found out Pedro had lost.

"Who said anything about losing?" Sarah said. "You mean my mom and me went to Staples for nothing?"

They were on her bedroom floor, surrounded by poster boards, Magic Markers, even a digital photo of the two of them that Sarah's mom had taken and had blown up at the copy store.

They were going to put it on the poster with this written below it:

"Pedro and Sarah. A Winning Team."

Sarah was doing the lettering herself. She was as good and neat with lettering as she was at everything else—soccer and lacrosse and girls' basketball and playing the guitar. And studying for history tests. If Ned was Mr. Everything at their school, she was *Miss* Everything.

She looked up now from her work centering another picture on another board before she glued it and said, "You want me to change this to *losing team*?"

Pedro forced up a smile. Usually smiling came naturally to him when he was with Sarah.

He knew he could talk about stuff with her, open up more than he ever did with Joe, Jamal or Bobby. Even though he'd never admit this to his guy friends, talking the way he did with her didn't seem like such a bad thing.

"Can I just say I'm trying to keep it real, the way Jamal does?" he said.

"No," she said. "First of all, nobody talks as cool as Jamal does. And second, you promised all of us that you were going to lose all the talk about losing, and now you're over here and that's *all* you're talking about."

"Okay," Pedro said. "I should've said *if* we lose."

Sarah didn't say anything now. She just put down the glue and stared at him, the way you did when you were trying to get the other person to blink first.

"What's really going on here?" she said.

"Nothing."

"Something," she said. "You want to tell me something."

"No I don't."

Sarah said, "Yes, you do."

"You don't know everything about me," Pedro said.

She didn't say anything now, just raised an eyebrow and gave him a look that said, *Oh, really?*

Pedro couldn't help himself. He laughed for the first time all night and said, "I give up."

Then he told her what had happened at practice, the way Ned had messed with him, had gone out of his way to let everybody know how well he thought Dave DeLuca was doing at point guard every time Dave was on his team.

The way Pedro thought—no, was sure—he was being punished in basketball for running against Ned in the school election.

When he finished, Sarah said, "What does Joe think? He's almost as smart as I am on the subject of you."

"He just said I had a lousy night because I was trying too hard," Pedro said. "And that the harder I tried the lousier I got."

"Possible?"

"No," Pedro said. "I mean, it's not *im*possible. I did have a bad night, and that's on me. All

I'm saying is that I had help. I know Ned's game and he knows mine, and that's why I know what was going on."

Before Sarah could say anything, Pedro added this: "And I know that if this election is going to wreck up my basketball season, I'm not doing it. You can run for president and get Jamal or Bobby to run with you."

He expected her to get mad. Or throw one of her famous arm punches. Or—much worse— pinch him on the upper arm the way she did when something *really* dumb came out of his mouth.

She gave him her very best smile instead.

"We both know that is the wrong speech, Mr. President," she said.

"What does that mean?"

Sarah said, "It means we're in this together, and I'm not quitting and you're not either."

"I can't have him against me at school and in basketball."

"Listen," Sarah said. "If you say he's doing that to you in basketball, I believe you. I always believe you. But you can't let that beat you. And *we* are not going to let *them* beat us." Now she pulled her fist back, like she was going to throw a big punch, and poked him lightly in the middle of his chest with a finger instead. "I don't like to lose at anything."

"That's because you never do," Pedro said. "You really are the Ned of girls."

"You don't like to lose any more than I do."

The next thing came out so loud it surprised him. "Tell me what to do about this!" he said.

"What you always do," Sarah said. "Work harder."

"You sound like my dad."

Sarah smiled again and said, "That is the nicest thing you have ever said to me, Mr. Morales."

"Sarah," he said. "Ned isn't just the best player on our team. He's the best player in town and the best player in our league."

"He's better than you at basketball," Sarah said. "But you're better than *him*, especially if he's acting this way. And you're going to prove it."

EIGHT

By the second week of practice, Dave DeLuca was getting as much time with the first team as Pedro was.

Sometimes more.

Coach Cory told Pedro not to get discouraged, he was just "mixing and matching" at this point, and that right now the offense just seemed to be "clicking" better when Ned and Dave were out there together.

Making it all sound like no big deal when they both knew that it was.

"You know you're still my guy, right?" Coach Cory said.

"Sure," Pedro said, knowing he sounded about as sincere as he felt. He didn't feel like the coach's guy, didn't feel like the guy he used to be on a basketball court.

"Hey," Coach Cory said. "You know how good I am at spreading the minutes around."

Yeah, Pedro thought. *My minutes.*

If you weren't Pedro Morales, if you didn't know what was really going on, you wouldn't have known anything had changed between Ned and him. Or with their team. But Pedro knew. He could see how different Ned was when Dave was out there with him, the way Ned tried to feature him every chance he could and went out of his way to give Dave a chance to shine.

The spotlight that Pedro always felt was trained on Ned? It was as if Ned was turning it around and putting it on Dave DeLuca.

Dave wasn't as good a point guard as Pedro. He couldn't pass as well, didn't see the court as well, really could only dribble with his right hand, and was an even worse outside shooter than Pedro was.

None of that mattered lately, because Ned made sure it didn't. If you could play at all—and you had to be able to play to make this team—he could make you look good if he wanted to. If he wanted you to look bad? Same.

Now it was as if he had gone ahead and changed the starting lineup without saying a word to anybody about it, not even the coach.

Coach Cory liked to say that there were always five or six plays that could change a game. An open guy who didn't get the pass. Or make the shot. A rebound that that a defensive guy should have had, but which ended up in the hands of one of the offensive guys. A missed layup. A loose ball that you ended up with instead of the other guys.

"The biggest stories in sports are really a bunch of small moments," Coach liked to say. "Sometimes one moment."

He even used baseball as his big example. He talked about how the greatest comeback in sports history—when the Red Sox came back from three games to none against the Yankees in the 2004 American League Championship Series—started this way in the ninth inning of Game 4, when the Yankees were three outs away from the World Series:

A walk.

A stolen base.

A single up the middle.

"All that did was tie the game," Coach Cory said. "And the Yankees were still up three games to zip. But they were done from that moment on, we just didn't know it until a few days later. Hugest story ever, and how did it start? Walk, stolen base, a single up the middle."

The point of this, he always told them, was that you'd better play every play as hard as you could, because it could be the one that changed everything.

Right now, Pedro couldn't make a play to save his life. And that's why he knew, without Coach Cory coming out and saying it, that when the season started against Camden on Sunday afternoon, it was going to start with him on the bench.

Didn't mean he was going to stay there. Didn't mean it was permanent. He was still going to get his minutes, and his own chance to shine this season. He was still trying as hard as he could, as hard as he ever had.

It was just that nothing was clicking for him right now.

His favorite season of the year wasn't spring or summer or fall. It was *basketball* season. Now it was here and it had gone wrong for him before it even started, and he couldn't get the idea out of his head that it had *really* started to go wrong when he made the decision to run for class president.

The day before the season opener was a Saturday, which meant soccer in the park with his dad.

His dad had been spending even more time than usual at Casa Luis as the date of the restaurant's opening grew closer. Once again, Pedro had told him that he could skip soccer if he was too busy.

"Soccer with you keeps me fit," his dad said on their way to the field. "Probably because it makes me so happy."

So they played the way they always had, and for a couple of hours, Pedro was able to forget about basketball, throwing himself into his other sport, trying to keep up with his dad, trying to make sure he seemed as happy today as on all the other Saturdays.

But when they had finished, and were walking the length of the field toward the parking lot, Luis Morales said, "Something is bothering you today."

Forget about reading his mind. Pedro's dad was able to read his son's heart.

"I'm fine, Papa."

"No, you are not. Is it school, or sports?"

Pedro wanted to tell him it was both, wanted to tell him in the worst way. He didn't want to hold back anymore, because he had never held back anything from his dad—at least not anything important.

But he still wasn't ready to tell him about the election.

He thought of another one of his dad's expressions, one from his job, the one about half the loaf being better than none. So he gave his dad half the story now.

"Sports," he said.

"What about sports?"

"Things aren't going so good with my team," Pedro said.

He stopped now in the middle of the field, looking around him as he did, thinking that everything looked the same as it had the Saturday morning when he had made up his mind to run for class president. The sun was high in the sky, but still the air was a little cooler today. The feel of the grass underneath his soccer spikes was the same as it always was. And they'd run and laughed and chased the ball and each other the way they always did on Saturday mornings.

But Pedro knew that things had changed so much in a couple of weeks.

Even if he was the only one who actually knew how much.

"But it's opening day tomorrow!" his dad said, clapping him on the back. "And in sports, opening day is always supposed to feel like a holiday, is it not?"

"I'm playing like *Cepillín*," he said to his dad.

He was a famous clown from a television show in Mexico, *El Show de Cepillín,* which Luis Morales used to watch when he was a boy.

"This I do not believe," his dad said. "Basketball is not just your favorite sport, as much as it pains me to say that. It is also your best. You have a gift, son."

"Not this season."

"There is no season yet, there is just practice."

"Papa," Pedro said, "I'm not starting tomorrow's game."

"But you started last year. You always start."

"This isn't last year."

"What happened?"

"I stink now, that's what happened."

"You don't stink at anything," his dad said. "Not your whole life."

Pedro thought: *In his eyes, I'm Ned*.

"You haven't seen our practices," Pedro said. "It's like I've forgotten how to play."

The other night, he even shot an air ball from the free throw line when he had a chance to win a scrimmage for his team.

The two of them stopped now, at the goal closest to the parking lot. His dad's eyes were on

Pedro now, somehow dark and bright at the same time.

"Is there something more that you are not telling me?"

Pedro put a smile between them, almost like he was using it to play defense.

"No, just that I pretty much stink."

His dad said, "Why do you sound so beaten before an official game is even played? And I do not just mean beaten out of a starting job for now."

"Dave's playing better than me."

"For now."

"Papa, sometimes it's like I can't get out of my own way."

"But you will."

"How can you be so sure of that?"

In a quiet voice, not joking now, his dad said, "Because you are my son. Because you are a Morales. And in the Morales family, we believe that anything is possible."

He sounded so sure. As sure as Sarah had sounded when she told Pedro he was better than Ned. As sure as Joe had sounded when he said that Pedro was the coolest kid in class, that Pedro was the one who should be class president.

Then his dad was clapping him on the back, telling him again, for what felt like the thousandth time in Pedro's life, about what it was like when he first set foot on American soil as a teenager. That if you set your heart and your mind to something, nobody could beat you, and that when you got knocked down you got back up, because that was the real measure of someone's talent and heart and character and spirit.

"Nobody can stop you," his dad said.

Nobody except Ned Hancock, Pedro thought.

His dad was still talking when they got into the car and began to drive away from the school, like this was part of the same speech he had given that day about "President Morales."

Only today, Pedro wasn't listening.

NINE

Pedro wore No. 10.

It wasn't because any of his favorite NBA players wore that number—Steve Nash, his main man, wore No. 13 for the Suns—but because his dad had worn No. 10 when he played soccer as a boy in Mexico, and wore it still in what he called his league of old men.

So Pedro was 10 this season the same as he had been on the fifth-grade team.

Back when he was still a starter.

But he wasn't a starter today at Vernon High School. The gym looked exactly as it did for varsity games, with the bleachers pulled out from the side walls, new scoreboards brightly lit behind both baskets, and a scorers' table set up at half-court, where one parent kept the official stat book and another one operated the clock.

Pedro's mom and dad—and Sarah—were in the stands with the rest of the Vernon parents, behind the Knights' bench. The Camden parents sat at the other end. Last season, Vernon had lost to the Camden Cavaliers in the league semi-finals, and Pedro recognized a lot of the kids on their team. The two best were Tim Barnicle, their starting point guard, and Alex Truba, a tall, skinny Cuban-American boy who played small forward the same as Ned did.

Alex didn't have the all-around game that Ned did, but he was the best outside shooter Camden had, even from beyond the high school three-point line, and if you got up on him as a way of taking away his shot, he could put the ball on the floor with either hand and drive to the basket.

In the huddle right before the game, Coach Cory said to Ned, "You remember Truba's philosophy about shooting. Guy thinks that the greatest tragedy in basketball is to be hot and not know it."

Ned laughed along with everybody else. "I hear you, Coach," Ned said. "If his hands are on the ball, his first thought is shooting."

"And second," Joe said. "And third."

"Now as for my point guard . . . " Coach Cory said.

For a second, almost like a reflex, Pedro thought Coach was talking to him.

He wasn't.

"I'm here, Coach," Dave said.

"You have to stay in front of that young man wearing number one for them," Coach Cory said. That meant Tim Barnicle. "Because if he can break *you* down off the dribble, that's gonna be the same as breaking *us* down."

Dave nodded to let Coach know he understood. Then Coach Cory had them all put their hands together in the middle of the huddle, and told them the same thing he'd told them before every game last season.

"Before the ref throws the ball up, take a look in the stands, and know there isn't an adult here who wouldn't change places with you," Coach said. "Who wouldn't want to be eleven again and have a chance to be playing a game like this today? Now get out there and honor the opportunity."

Pedro watched the starting five—Ned, Dave, Jeff, Jamal, and Joe—take the court, and thought: *It's a lot easier to honor that opportunity when you're starting.*

He took the last seat at the end of their bench, not wanting to sit next to Coach and look as if he were too eager to get in there. He felt a little bit like he'd been told to go sit by himself in an empty classroom after school. He wasn't going to pout. He told himself he was going to cheer on his teammates every chance he got. He had always been a fast learner at sports, the guy who picked up the new play faster than anybody else on the team—except maybe Ned.

So this was one more thing he would have to learn: how to be a scrub.

He didn't even want to look across the court to where his parents and Sarah were sitting.

Pedro told himself that he'd only do that after he'd gotten into the game and actually done something.

The Knights didn't miss him at all in the first quarter, because they came out flying. They couldn't do anything wrong and the Cavaliers couldn't do anything right.

The Knights played so well that Pedro, as much of a team guy as he was, started to feel even worse about being on the bench. It was like: *Do they have to make it look this easy without me on the court?*

It was as if the Knights were pitching a perfect game. And the biggest reason was that the ball seemed to be in Ned Hancock's hands as often as if he was the one pitching.

When the Knights ran their offense, they seemed to end up with layups half the time. When they ran out on the break, the Cavs were so slow trying to keep up, it was as if they were wearing their winter boots.

Dave was shutting down his man, Tim, staying in front of him the way Coach Cory had told him to. Ned was doing everything to Alex Truba except pulling his jersey up over his head to blindfold him.

When Jeff Harmon drove to the basket for

yet one more layup right before the horn ended the first quarter, the Knights were ahead by the amazing score of 22–2. Before they even got to the bench, Coach Cory was out on the court to meet them, telling them not to go into their version of a touchdown dance, because there were three quarters left to play.

Then he turned back to the bench and said, "Next five, let's go."

Bobby Murray said, "Oh, great. How do we top that?"

"We don't," Pedro said in a voice only loud enough for Bobby to hear. "I think only Duke or Carolina could do that."

Pedro was always nervous when he first got into a game. Not because he was scared of making a mistake, though there was always a little bit of that going on inside him. No. Usually Pedro had what Coach Cory liked to call his "good nerves" going for him. Nerves that Coach said you could always make disappear with your first good pass, good shot, or good stop on defense.

Today he couldn't make them go away.

He wasn't exactly playing badly. And the second unit—that expression had never bothered him before, but now he hated the sound of it inside his head: *second* unit, like it was a way of saying second class—would hold their own against the Cavaliers.

It wasn't that.

It was that Pedro felt as if some stranger were wearing No. 10 today.

Pedro was the opposite of what he usually was, in soccer or basketball, which meant that he wasn't playing to make something happen. Worse than that, he was playing afraid.

Afraid to make a mistake.

And if you were afraid like that, you shouldn't even be out there.

He'd see an opening, a chance to thread the needle with one of his bullet passes. And he wouldn't take it, because he was afraid he'd throw the ball away.

All of a sudden, a turnover felt like the thing that scared him most in the world. He was still seeing plays develop inside his head; he just wasn't doing anything about them. And in a way, a big way, playing the game like that was worse than watching it from the bench.

With about two minutes left in the half, Pedro was on the right side of the court, just outside the circle, when Clarence set a perfect pick for Bobby over on the weak side. Pedro saw the whole thing developing, and even though there was some traffic between him and Bobby's lane to the basket, the pass was there.

It was *there*.

But Pedro waited too long, held the ball, even though he could feel Bobby's eyes burning into him the whole time. Finally he just swung the ball over to Clarence, who seemed so surprised to get it that he fired up a shot that banged high off the backboard.

As they were running down the court getting back on defense, Bobby made sure to run past Pedro. "Dude," he said, "what just happened there?"

"Thought Alex was reading my eyes," Pedro said.

"But I *had* him," Bobby said.

"Just couldn't pull the trigger," Pedro said, then acted as if he were looking around for his man.

Bobby wouldn't let it go.

"I saw that," Bobby said. "What I'm not getting here is why."

The half ended with the Knights still comfortably ahead, 36–20. Out of the corner of his eye Pedro could see his dad stand up as the Knights ran past that part of the bleachers toward their locker room. Pedro could even hear him clapping harder than anybody around him.

He kept his head down and kept running, thinking that if Luis Morales was cheering the way Pedro had just played, then it really was official that he could do no wrong in his dad's eyes.

The second half felt more like a scrimmage than a real game. The Knights' lead got back to twenty points and pretty much stayed there no matter who Coach Cory had in the game.

He pulled Ned and Dave about four minutes into the third quarter, and put Pedro back in. He told him to make sure to work the ball on of-

fense, and even to run through plays twice sometimes as a way of not running up the score.

In one huddle he told the guys, "There's a
way to take it easy on them without making it
look as if we are. You hearing me on this?"

Everybody nodded.

"This isn't college football," he said, grinning.
"We're not trying to win by fifty so we can move
up in the polls."

Even if he could find his old game somehow,
Pedro knew he couldn't really play it. Couldn't
be what Steve Nash was, what Chris Paul was,
what all the great point guards were: creators.

The Knights were making the extra pass now
as a way of *not* getting an easy basket, passing
just to keep passing. It was basketball about as
much fun as diagramming sentences in English
class.

Pedro scored a couple of baskets on layups,
and got a couple of assists to Joe when he would
have looked stupid not passing him the ball underneath the basket. He even played the last two
minutes of the game with Ned, both of them hav-

ing been told by Coach Cory to feed the ball to Jamal, the one guy on the Knights who'd had a terrible shooting day.

"I don't want J walking out of here feeling bad about himself on a day when we had such a good win," Coach said.

So Ned passed it to Jamal for a baby hook which he made, and Pedro fed him a bounce pass that produced a layup.

On their last possession, Jamal got a rebound and kicked it out to Ned on the left side. Pedro, going on instinct, cut toward the middle. Like they were starting one of their three-man weaves. And for one moment, basketball felt fun again for him.

They hadn't been running fast breaks the whole fourth quarter, but as Pedro caught the pass from Ned, he was running right at Coach Cory, who made a waving motion with his hand, like he was telling them to go ahead and let it rip one last time.

Pedro did.

He led the break now. Ned had cut behind

him and gotten out on his right. Jamal was on his left. Pedro threw it to Ned, who threw it back to him. Then Pedro gave it back to Jamal.

Now I'm playing, Pedro thought. *Even if it's just one play.*

Pedro's plan was to let Jamal finish, have him go hard to the basket and finish strong. He threw it to Ned one more time, knowing he would throw it back, as the two Camden kids who were back on defense pinched over toward him when he got the ball again.

Only the ball didn't make it back to Pedro, even though Ned was eyeballing him the whole time.

Grinning at him, even.

His eyes stayed on Pedro as he put the ball down on a right-hand dribble, then whipped this amazing bounce pass off the dribble and past the defenders, the ball catching Jamal in perfect stride, and Jamal laying it up with his left hand as the horn ending the game sounded.

Everybody in the Knights' cheering section jumped up, and the Knights on the court went running for Ned as if his assist had won the game by a single basket.

Pedro went over and joined them, because the whole team was over there now. He was still a team guy, even though the game had ended the way it had begun for him—with him feeling like a spectator.

TEN

"Legit now," Pedro said to Joe. "You really don't see what's been going on?"

It was an hour after the Camden game and they were at Carinor Park, both Pedro and Joe still in the Knights hoodies they'd been given as part of this year's uniforms. They were shooting around, trying to get a little more ball in before it got too dark, neither one of them feeling as if they'd played a full game.

"All I'm seeing," Joe said, "is that you're not playing your game."

"Because I *can't*," Pedro said. "That's the thing."

"Dude," Joe said, "you're starting to sound totally wack about Ned. Like, I get it that you're running against him for president, but that doesn't mean he's turned into a *Saw* movie all by himself."

They had started a game of Around the World and Pedro couldn't even get past the right corner, his first stop. He missed his first shot, then chanced it and missed his second.

"Great," he said, slamming the ball down after he retrieved it. "I'm gonna do as good here as I did in the game."

"We did *win* the game, right?" Joe said.

"No thanks to me."

"You act like you missed ten shots and had ten turnovers," Joe said. "And like Ned never passed you the rock once, only that's not the way it was."

"He wants Dave to start and he wants me on the bench, whether you see that or not."

"I'm not telling you this as just your teammate now," Joe said. "I'm telling you as your friend. You gotta let this go."

Joe was moving around the court as they talked, moving from point to point in their game, making one shot after another even though shooting was never his best thing. Usually on days like this Pedro loved coming over to Carinor, just goofing around, replaying the game they'd just played, not wanting the basketball part of the day to end until it absolutely had to.

But today was different.

Pedro sensed it, and he knew Joe sensed it. They were just going through the motions. And Pedro couldn't help himself. He was getting madder and madder that Joe was either too blind to see what was really going on with Ned, or too stubborn to admit it.

"You say you're my friend," Pedro said. "So why don't you start acting like it?"

Joe was in the left corner now, two shots from winning the game, but instead of shooting, he just put the ball down and walked over to Pedro.

When he was close, in that quiet voice of his, he said, "What did you just say?"

Joe had walked over, but Pedro knew he was the one who had crossed a line.

Joe Sutter liked to say that the best thing about best friends was that they could say just about any stupid thing that came into their heads.

Just not this stupid.

"All I meant is, you know me," Pedro said, "and you know I don't make stuff up."

"I don't know you today," Joe said, staring at him.

Pedro didn't say anything.

"I *am* your friend," Joe said. "And you know it. You're big on telling the truth. Me too, and so here it is. If you don't stop blaming Ned for the way you're playing, you can forget about ever getting your starting job back."

Pedro could feel the back of his neck getting hot all over again.

"I'm out of here," he said.

"Fine with me," Joe said.

He started walking toward the street, the ball in the corner where he'd left it. Pedro went over and picked it up. He couldn't help himself, so he fired up one last shot.

Air ball.

After dinner he went down to the basement to watch the Suns play the Hornets on ESPN, knowing that at least down there basketball would still be fun, just because Nash and Paul were in the same game.

It was always a high score when these two teams played, both of them acting as if there was a ten-second shot clock in the pros instead of a twenty-four-second clock, both teams pushing the ball every chance they got.

Luis Morales had gotten TiVo for the big screen in the basement, and sometimes Pedro felt like he was wearing it out, rewinding one fast break after another, just to make sure his eyes weren't playing tricks on him when Nash or Paul had the ball.

But even his favorite point guards couldn't get him out of his bad mood tonight. Pedro kept replaying his whole day, felt like he was using TiVo on everything that had happened to him— not just in the Knights-Cavaliers game, but also with him and Joe at Carinor Park.

I don't know you, Joe had said.

It made Pedro mad all over again, but not because Joe was wrong.

Pedro didn't even know himself right now.

"Hey."

He turned around and saw his mom standing at the bottom of the stairs, a big bowl of popcorn in her hands.

She was smiling.

"Since Dad's working late," she said, "I decided to send myself into the game."

Pedro said, "You always tell me that the only basketball game you're interested in is one I'm playing."

"Well," she said, taking the other end of the couch, placing the bowl on the coffee table, "that *is* technically true. But tonight your old mom just got the feeling that you could use a little company down here in the boys club."

His mom didn't miss much.

"Mom," Pedro said, "you don't have to keep me company. I'm okay."

"I didn't say you weren't."

On the TV screen, the announcers were all excited because Chris Paul had just dribbled down the baseline, gone underneath the basket, then somehow wheeled when he got into the deep corner and threw a pass out to the opposite wing, where David West was standing all alone to make a three-pointer.

"How did he see the other player all the way over there?" Anna Morales said.

"Chris Paul has eyes in the back of his head," Pedro said.

"You know what *my* eyes are telling me?" she said.

That was the way it worked with her. Pedro knew this was coming from the time she'd showed up with the popcorn. She was closing in like a slick defender cutting off the court on him.

"What?" he said.

"That my boy isn't acting like someone whose team won the game today."

"Is it that obvious?"

"Yes," she said. "It is."

He turned around so he was facing her. "I just feel like I got worse between last season and now," he said. "And when I got out there today . . . " He reached up with his right hand like he was trying to find the right words in the air between them. "When I got out there today I was just . . . *lost*."

"Is it because you didn't get to start?"

Pedro sighed. "Not being in the starting lineup, that was just the start of it. Even when I was in the game I didn't really feel like I was in it."

"Your dad said the same thing."

"He did?"

"He said you weren't . . . something." Now she was the one searching for the right word, until she smiled again, in triumph. "*Involved!* He said you weren't involved and he said you weren't getting the other players involved the way you usually do."

"Papa was right. As usual."

"But he said he wasn't worried about you, that you'd figure it out."

"I'm not so sure."

"Your dad says that when a door closes in front of you, you find a way to get it open. Or you just kick it down."

"I feel more like a door got slammed in my face today."

He knew he had to stop now, because if he tried to tell her more he would have to tell her all of it. And if Joe didn't get what was going on, how could his mom?

He said, "Tell Dad not to worry, I'll figure it out."

He turned himself back so he was facing the television set, hoping that would be a sign to her that they were done talking about this for now.

Only he had said the wrong thing.

"Your dad's got enough to worry about these days," she said.

"What does that mean?" Pedro said. "Is something wrong at the restaurant?"

"Nothing he can't fix," she said. "You know your dad. He thinks he can fix everything except the weather."

"That's because he can."

"It's just that the owner of his old restaurant isn't being so nice these days," she said. "Your dad thought everybody at Miller's would be happy for him. But now as he gets closer to his opening, he doesn't think they're so happy to have the competition. Too many people come in and ask him when Luis's place is going to open."

Pedro hit the mute button on the remote.

"So what are they doing?"

"One of the waiters who was going to come with your dad, Mr. Miller raised his salary and made him maitre d'. And he raised the salary of one of the bartenders. When your dad asked Mr. Miller about it, he said, 'That's business,' and hung up the phone. And then one of the carpenters he was using suddenly stopped showing up for work."

"Papa will find other people."

"He will," she said. "This has still hurt him, I can tell." She paused and a sad look came into her eyes. "Someday you'll find out for yourself, how sometimes you think you know people when you really don't know them at all."

I don't have to wait, Pedro thought, *I'm finding out already.*

It was halftime of the Suns game by now, and Pedro's bedtime. He pointed the remote at the set, shutting it off, and picked up the bowl of popcorn that the two of them had emptied as they talked.

"You know your dad," his mom said. "He won't complain, he'll just work harder."

They both headed up the stairs, Pedro thinking that even when his dad wasn't in the room, he was still there for him. The way his mom had been there for him tonight, more than she even knew.

Because she was right. His dad never whined or complained about anything. And even if Mr. Miller, his old boss, had hurt him, he knew his dad wasn't going to waste any time feeling sorry for himself.

From now on, Pedro thought, *neither am I.*

By the time he got up to his room, he'd made up his mind about something: His season hadn't started today.

It was starting tomorrow night when he got to practice.

He was going to make sure one thing hadn't changed, no matter how much his basketball team had. He was going to make sure that he was still his father's son.

ELEVEN

If you watched Ned Hancock at school, even watched him closely, you would have thought nothing had changed between him and Pedro.

Pedro didn't buy it for a second, because everything had changed in the gym, whether anybody else noticed it or not. They weren't even close to being the one-two punch they used to be, the two players out there who really seemed to read each other's minds, Pedro being the one kid who was able to see the same things Ned did on a basketball court.

Yet in school, things looked exactly as they always had. Maybe it was because there were more people watching. Pedro was starting to think that Ned was as good at being a phony as he was at sports and everything else.

"You know what's cool about this election?" Ned asked him in math class on Monday morning.

Mrs. Mahoney had paired them up in the kind of competition she'd sometimes have to keep things interesting. Today she just wanted to see which two-person team could solve a page of problems the fastest.

What's cool? Pedro thought. *How about nothing?*

"You tell me," he said.

"It's like we're running this long race," Ned said, "except nobody knows who's ahead."

Pedro saw his opening and decided to take it. "Just so long as things are still cool between us, no matter who wins the race."

Ned looked at Pedro as if he had turned into a problem that needed to be solved. "Why wouldn't they be? Cool between us, I mean."

Before Pedro could say anything, Mrs. Mahoney asked if everybody was ready. She was about to start the clock, and the winners got to skip their homework assignments tonight.

"C'mon, let's do this," Ned said. "The way we do it on the court."

What a guy.

That night, Pedro was wearing his new attitude like it was his practice jersey, hustling all over the court, hustling more than he usually did. Like he was trying to make the team all over again.

Getting after it the way Luis Morales' son was supposed to.

If he was going to come off the bench, he was going to come off it as hard as he could. Once he was out there, he was going to play *his* game— his usual game, his old game—even if that meant having to work around the great Ned Hancock.

Pedro hadn't meant anything personal when he'd decided to challenge Ned in the election. It was really more of a way for Pedro to challenge himself. And an opportunity to show his mom and dad—his dad, especially—that he believed in all the ideals about America that his dad had been preaching to him his whole life: that America was the capital of possibilities.

The problem wasn't his ego.

It was Ned's.

It was Ned who had made the whole thing personal. And Pedro knew it was time to fight back. Big-time.

It was probably why even Joe was looking at him funny that night, as if he didn't recognize the Pedro who was trying to be everywhere at once, diving for loose balls, even flying in from the outside to crash the boards sometimes.

During a water break, Coach Cory came over and said he couldn't decide whether this was the old Pedro or a new Pedro.

"The old one," Pedro said to him quietly. "Maybe just with a new attitude."

He wanted the ball in his hands on offense again, whether he was playing with Ned or not. He pushed the ball up the court every chance he got, and if his teammates didn't want to run with him, well, they just got left behind.

A couple of times he threaded the needle on passes—one to Bobby, one to Clarence—when he would have been better off holding the ball and not taking the chance.

Right before the end of their scrimmage, first unit against the second unit, the game tied at nine baskets all, Ned's team had the ball and a chance to win.

Like last ups in baseball.

Ned had the ball in the right corner and was starting to back in toward the basket. It never mattered whether Ned had his back to the basket or not, because he had his own eyes in the back of his head, same as Steve Nash. All the great passers did.

I have them too, Pedro thought, *even though I haven't been using them much lately.*

When Ned turned his head this time, Pedro knew exactly what was going to happen next. Just knew.

He could still read the guy's mind, read him like a book. He knew Ned was going to turn and whip a pass all the way over to the other wing where Jeff Harmon was set up for a wide-open three.

Like Nash the other night.

Pedro was guarding Dave, who'd run down into the opposite corner as a decoy. But Pedro wasn't worried about Dave now, and left him where he was in the corner as he ran the baseline toward Ned, ran it like a streak of light before anybody realized he was coming up behind Ned Hancock.

Pedro came in behind as Ned took one more dribble, and he slapped the ball away, picked him clean. Then he gathered the ball up before it went out of bounds, took off down the sideline before anybody on the first unit was quick enough to make the transition to defense, and made the easy layup that won the scrimmage for the second unit.

Before the ball was through the net and to the floor, Coach Cory blew his whistle and started clapping his hands, saying, "*That's* the way you play defense. Uh-*huh*!"

Then he turned to Ned, shrugged and said, "Even *you* got to protect the rock, Mr. Hancock."

Nobody said a word.

Pedro wasn't sure everybody was even *breathing*. Even in a nice way, Coach Cory had never called out Ned Hancock.

For anything.

The moment didn't last, because Coach was never quiet for very long. He told them to shoot around for the last fifteen minutes until pick-up time, and to start thinking about the Sherrill game on Saturday.

Only then did the gym sound like a gym again: balls bouncing, players scattering to find open baskets, the real ones at both ends or the ones on the side.

Everybody seemed to be in motion except Ned.

He was still standing where he'd been when Pedro stole the ball from him, with his arms at his sides, staring at Pedro.

He was supposed to be the most unselfish, un-cocky player in town, but now he was looking at Pedro the same way he had the day he found out Pedro was running for president against him.

Like nobody else was even supposed to be breathing his air.

Like he was showing Pedro the real Ned Hancock again.

This time Pedro stared right back at him,

held Ned's look and held his ground at the same time, let him know that he wasn't going anywhere.

Pedro looked down the court at Ned Hancock as if to say, *I'm here.*

TWELVE

The Knights won again on Saturday, on the road against Sherrill, a town about fifteen minutes away. They had taken the lead in the first quarter and never lost it, though the second unit did let Sherrill come back and tie them up a minute before halftime. But then Bobby hit two shots from the outside, one of them a three-pointer, and everybody on the second unit walked off the court feeling as if they'd done their jobs, pretty much held their place.

Pedro wasn't great, despite all the good intentions he'd brought with him to Sherrill. A few times, in his determination to start making things happen again, he forced passes and caused turn-overs.

He didn't care. His attitude was that when

he saw an opening, he wasn't going to let it go. He was through playing scared.

In the end, he wound up with more assists than turnovers, including assists on both of Bobby's baskets. And even though outside shooting remained the weakest part of his game, Pedro had even managed to sink a three-pointer of his own.

For the first time this season, he felt as if he'd helped the team more than he'd hurt it.

Ned, of course, was playing like a total star, at both ends of the court, dominating the game in almost every possible way when he was out there. He wasn't just making Dave look better today, he was making everybody around him look better, maybe even making the *Knights* look better than they really were. And as soon as he got back out to start the third quarter, the Knights' lead went from five points to ten in what seemed like a blink.

With five minutes to go in the quarter, Coach Cory took out Dave and put Pedro in at the point. So this was different than the second half of the Camden game, when Pedro and Ned had only played together during what the announcers loved to call "garbage time" at the end of blow-out NBA games.

This was real ball now. Even though they still had a nice cushion, Coach Cory told them during a time-out to "put these suckers away."

For a few minutes, the five on the court were last year's starting lineup from the fifth-grade team: Pedro, Ned, Joe, Jamal, and Bobby. Maybe things were getting back to normal after all. That's what Pedro thought, mostly because that's what he wanted to believe.

Badly.

And for those last few minutes of the third quarter, it was like they were all in sync again, sharing the ball, keeping their lead even though Sherrill's best player, a kid named Dwan, who was built like a football tight end but had a sweet shooting touch from the outside, was doing his best to keep his team in the game.

The Knights were in charge, though, and had been in charge for most of the game. Everybody in Sherrill's tiny, old-fashioned middle school gym knew it.

They only had a few set plays, with a couple of options for each one. And while most of them technically started with the point guard making the first pass, the plays *really* started with the point forward.

Ned.

So even with Dwan staying hot, the Sherrill Sonics never pulled closer than eight points. And everyone on the court knew that Ned would never let them pull closer than that.

Maybe that was why he decided it was safe to start playing puppet master again with a minute to go in the quarter.

Sherrill had gone into a zone by then. Pedro had the ball up on top, Ned over on the right wing and Bobby on the left. When the Knights went to a 3-2 offense like this, Joe and Jamal would take turns coming out from under the basket, setting up at the foul line.

They were working a little clock now, passing the ball around, all five of them getting touches, all five knowing that Coach Cory was loving life as they did, especially because they hadn't practiced much against a zone.

The ball was a blur now, moving that fast, from Pedro to Ned and then back to Pedro and into the post and back out and over to Bobby and then back around the horn.

Finally, when Ned was alone on the right side, everybody else having cleared out, he clapped his hands.

Pedro knew what that meant from last season. It wasn't a designed play, just one he and Ned Hancock used to run all the time. Just the two of them. Usually when you clapped your hands on offense, it meant you wanted the ball. Only Pedro knew Ned didn't want it on the wing. Pedro was supposed to fake a two-hand pass, and as soon as he did, Ned would cut for the basket. Even against a zone it would work like a charm. Most times the defense on Ned's side—having watched them pass the ball around on the outside—would get caught flat-footed and Ned would get an easy two.

Pedro faked the pass, like he always had in the past.

Ned took a step toward the basket.

As soon as he did, Pedro threw the ball where

he knew Ned was going to be, because he had always been there in the past.

Only Ned stopped, like a car jamming on the brakes.

It was too late for Pedro to stop. He was fully committed by then, so he threw the ball over the defense, over everybody, out of bounds, feeling as if he'd thrown it all the way out of the gym.

Pedro looked over to the bench and saw Coach Cory shake his head. Then he looked at the clock right next to Coach at the scorers' table and saw there were only twenty-five seconds left in the quarter.

So Pedro tried to set a new world's record for hustling back on defense. As he did, he heard Sherrill's coach call for one last shot.

Pedro had only one game plan then: Get up on his guy, get one stop, and get to the bench.

Sherrill worked the ball on the outside now until there were fifteen seconds left.

Then Pedro heard their coach yell, "*Go!*"

They had set up their own two-man game on the right side: Pedro's guy and Ned's guy, Dwan.

Pedro's guy dribbled over to the wing. Pedro

gave a quick look over his shoulder, saw that Dwan had stayed home for now. The Sonics had run this play a few times already. Dwan would make a move out of the corner as if coming out for a pick-and-roll. But then he'd plant and take off for the basket, like a classic back-door cut. If he wasn't open for a layup, he'd come all the way around to the other side and somebody would pick for him over there, and he'd put up another one from the outside.

Plenty of time to do that now.

Pedro stayed focused on his guy, locked on him, ready to swarm him as soon as he gave up his dribble.

Only the kid kept his dribble, put the ball hard on the floor and started to drive, making it look as if he was going to try to blow past Pedro and get around the corner.

So Pedro thought, anyway.

He thought wrong.

This time they *were* running a pick-and-roll, Dwan coming at full speed out of the corner like a runaway truck. At least that's the way Joe would describe the play for Pedro much later.

Pedro ran into Dwan's pick, got blindsided, as if he'd run into the side of a house. No one had called it out in time to warn him. It was always the responsibility of whoever's guy was setting the pick to warn his teammate. Ned had been on Dwan the whole game. He had to have seen it coming. Ned saw *everything* coming on the basketball court.

But Pedro saw none of this until it was too late, running hard in Dwan and getting absolutely smoked, his head hitting the floor as the buzzer sounded to end the quarter.

And, for Pedro, ending the game.

THIRTEEN

"I get it now," Joe said.

Pedro took the ice pack away from his head. "What was your first clue?" Pedro said. "When I went down like a bowling pin?"

They were in the basement at Pedro's house, Joe sitting on the floor playing video games, Pedro lying on the couch watching him.

Pedro put the ice pack back on his forehead.

"I'm just saying that I see what Ned's been doing, is all," Joe said.

"So let me get this straight," Pedro said, smiling. "Me getting bonked on the head knocked some sense into you?"

Joe smiled back. "I hadn't thought of it that way but, well, yeah."

• • •

Bobby Murray's mom was a doctor, and had been sitting with a lot of the other moms in the stands when Pedro's head made a sound on the floor like a wood bat hitting a baseball in the big leagues. As soon as Pedro went down, she was on the court so fast it was as if Coach Cory had subbed her into the game.

They brought him into a locker room, and Dr. Murray got her medical bag out of her car. She checked his eyes with a little flashlight, asked him to do some counting—by then Pedro was feeling good enough to say, "Uh-oh, math problems"— and finally told him that while he had taken a big knock, he didn't have a concussion. She told him to keep ice on the side of his forehead for the rest of the afternoon so he wouldn't look as if he'd lost a fight.

Pedro insisted on going back into the gym, so they let him. When he got to the bench during a time-out, he told Coach Cory he wanted to stay around and watch the end of the game. He checked the clock and saw that they were three minutes into the fourth quarter by then. Coach Cory put his hand on Pedro's shoulder, told him he'd already taken one for the team, to take the rest of the day off and he'd call to check in on him later.

When Pedro started to walk away, Ned walked with him. Pedro knew it was more for show than anything else, but there wasn't much he could do about it. So he just let it happen, let Ned look like a team leader walking him to the door.

"Sorry, dude," Ned said. "I should have called it out."

Pedro stopped, looked at him, said in a quiet voice, "You *think*?"

"Hey," Ned said, keeping his own voice down. "I made a mistake and I'm saying I'm sorry."

Acting like he was the injured party.

"No," Pedro said. "You're not."

Ned said, "You're saying I did it on purpose?"

"Everything you do on a basketball court has a purpose," Pedro said. "And one other thing: I'm not your dude anymore, *dude*."

He walked toward where his mom was waiting for him.

Now he was in the basement with Joe, his head starting to feel better, Anna Morales not coming down every ten minutes to ask how he was doing.

"How's the head really?" Joe said, not turning around, his eyes focused on *FIFA Soccer 08.*

"Great," Pedro said. "My mom stops asking and you start."

On the big screen, one of the players from Tottenham Hotspur—Joe always wanted to be Tottenham Hotspur, for no other reason than the cool name—scored a goal and Joe pumped his fist.

Even now, only half watching from the couch, Pedro couldn't believe how real the players on the screen looked, how real the action seemed. It was actually one of the things that Pedro liked best about playing video games: If you were smart enough and quick enough and good enough with the controller, you could make sports come out the way you wanted them to.

It was the way real sports were supposed to work, too.

Just not lately.

"What finally changed your mind?" Pedro said. "About Ned, I mean."

"When he clapped and then didn't move. He always cuts to the basket on that play. *Always*. And what happened later, that was just plain cold, dude. He always sees picks coming even before the other guy decides he wants to set one."

"Tell me about it," Pedro said.

"So the question is, what are we gonna do about it?"

"There's nothing for either one of us to do except play through this," Pedro said.

"What if we both go to Coach?"

"You know Coach," Pedro said. "He sees what he wants with Ned, and what he sees is Peter Perfect. The player who's gonna lead us to a perfect season. Hey, you saw it the other day when I stole the ball from Ned at practice. He says one little thing to Ned about protecting the ball and the other guys on the team act like he's grounded him for life or something."

"Word," Joe said.

Pedro sat down on the floor next to Joe now and grabbed the other controller.

Joe said, "Your mom said you had to keep the ice on until she told you to take it off."

Pedro said, "I can beat you one-handed *and* with a headache."

"Okay, I'm calling your mom," Joe said. "You're delirious."

"I did say something to him today," Pedro said.

Joe looked at him. "Ned?"

Pedro told him about their exchange right before he left the gym.

"You think you got through to him?" Joe said.

Pedro nodded. Slowly. "He knew what I was saying. And he's smart enough on hoops to know that *I* know what's been going on."

"Maybe the next time something happens you should get in his grill and just air him out in front of the whole team."

Pedro said he was going to air him out, just

not in the gym, and then told Joe when he was going to do it.

And where.

"Word," Joe said again, and put out his fist for a little pound.

"*Lots* of words," Pedro Morales said. "And the best kind."

"What kind is that?"

"The truth," Pedro said.

When he got home from school Monday afternoon he was surprised to find both his parents there.

His mom had taken the afternoon off from True Blue and his dad said he had just come from the restaurant to pick up some paperwork he had left in the tiny office he kept on the second floor of their house.

Usually Pedro liked to chill for a couple of hours between the end of school and the start of practice. Not today. As soon as he got home today he knew he just should have stayed at school, because he decided when he went upstairs to play video games that he wanted to be in the gym working on his shooting. But when he asked his mom to drive him to practice early, his dad said he'd take him instead.

"Let me go get my sneakers and we can go right now if you want," Luis Morales said.

"Why do you need your sneakers to drive me to school?"

"I could use a little exercise," his dad said, "that does not involve rearranging tables and opening boxes."

Then he ran up the stairs, taking them two at a time, the way Pedro did when he was impatient to go outside and play. When he came back down, Pedro said to him, "You don't have to do this, Papa."

"I want to," he said, then clapped his hands. "And who knows, maybe the old soccer dad can help you out with your basketball."

He put his arm around his son's shoulders and they walked through the front door together, like they were walking into one of their Saturday mornings.

• • •

But even having his dad on the court with him didn't help with his shot.

His dad kept rebounding the ball for him, telling him to trust it, boy, telling him just get a good look at the basket and then let it go.

Pedro still couldn't get nearly enough shots to fall.

"In soccer," Luis Morales said, "if you think too much, it is as if somebody keeps moving the goal."

He was right, as usual.

It was as if somebody kept moving the basket on Pedro, no matter how much his dad tried to keep him positive. And nobody he knew had a more positive attitude—about everything—than his dad did.

Pedro kept moving around the court, as if playing a game of Around the World against himself, trying to find a spot where he felt comfortable. But he couldn't. It seemed to be something different on every shot. He had too much air under the ball. Or not enough. He didn't put enough spin on the ball. Sometimes he felt as if he were chucking the ball from the side instead of taking his shooting hand right past his nose, the way Coach Cory had taught them on their very first day of fifth-grade practice.

The worse it got, the more frustrated Pedro became.

As good as his dad's attitude was, Pedro's was the opposite, at least today. This was something he couldn't blame on Ned Hancock or anybody else. His dad always liked to say that you couldn't fool sports, and so there was no point in trying to fool yourself.

Sports, Luis Morales said, always let you know exactly where you stood.

Today Pedro knew exactly where he stood with his shooting. No matter where he happened to be standing on the court.

"If I can't make these shots here, with nobody guarding me," he said to his dad, "how am I ever going to make a big shot in a game?"

"You will before the season goes much further, wait and see," his dad said, then snapped off an amazing bounce pass from all the way across the court, making Pedro wonder again what kind of player his dad could have been if he had had the chance to play basketball instead of soccer.

Pedro caught the ball chest-high just left of the free throw line, thought he had actually released one perfectly for a change, then saw that this was another one that was too hard and off-line, hitting high off the backboard without catching any iron.

"I quit!" Pedro shouted, his words seeming to bounce off every wall in the gym the way his shots had been bouncing around for the past hour.

He waved his dad off now, chased the ball down himself, placed it on the floor and soccer-kicked it as hard as he could toward the opposite end of the gym. Pedro was trying to kick it in the direction of the other basket, but hooked it badly so that it bounced off a tall stack of chairs.

Right to where Ned Hancock was standing.

Pedro had no idea how long Ned had been there or how much of his pathetic shooting display he'd seen. Just saw Ned calmly walk over, grab the ball, then throw a perfect football pass the length of the court.

Pedro didn't even have to move.

"Wow, dude," Ned called out, like they were best basketball buds still, Pedro thinking it was more for his dad's benefit than his own. "Now you can't even boot it straight."

FOURTEEN

Their next opponent was the Wilton Warriors, one of their big rivals.

No matter what sport you played in Vernon and no matter what your record was, your season wasn't a total loss if you could beat Wilton.

Now the Knights were getting the first of their two chances, the first game of a home-and-home series against the Warriors, the second game to be played in a week in Wilton.

Pedro knew what everybody else on their team knew: that the Warriors were 4–0, that they still hadn't lost as a group because they'd been undefeated champions of the league as fifth-graders, and that their backcourt of Kyle Sullivan and Nate Clark was already lighting up their league, same as last year.

Neither one of them was a pure point guard. Neither was a pure shooting guard. They could both pass, they could both put the ball on the floor, and they could both fill it up from the outside if they got even a sliver of daylight so small it was like it was trying to sneak through your blinds.

The Knights' guards were going to have to "man up" today—it was probably Coach Cory's favorite expression in the world—or the Warriors' two-year run as the best would continue.

"What we have here, gentlemen," Coach Cory said, "is an early-season contest with *serious* playoff implications."

Joe had mentioned once to Pedro that he sometimes thought that Coach Cory was like somebody from a foreign country who'd learned how to speak English watching *SportsCenter* on ESPN.

"To be the best," Coach Cory said in the locker room right before they went out the door, "you've got to beat the best."

Pedro was where he usually was at the start of the game—the far end of the Knights' bench.

Yet one thing was clear from the opening tip: Dave DeLuca had no chance against Nate Clark. Or Kyle Sullivan, when Coach switched Dave over to him. It was actually even worse with Kyle. When Dave backed off, Kyle hit from the perimeter. When Dave tried to crowd him, Kyle got to the basket so easily it was like he was wearing one of those E-ZPass gadgets that got you right through tollbooths.

Kyle was scoring at will. And frustrating Dave so much that he got two early fouls. Even as Pedro was kneeling next to Coach Cory, with Coach trying to get Dave out of there and get Pedro into the game, Dave managed to commit his third foul.

Coach Cory pushed Pedro toward the scorers' table, saying, "I don't care what you give me on offense today. But I want you to man up on *that* young man right now."

Meaning Kyle.

"Done," Pedro said.

"You know how we change games on this team, right?" Coach Cory said.

Pedro turned and nodded as the scorer blew

the horn, sending him into the game. "One stop at a time," Pedro said to his coach.

Pedro immediately stole the ball from Kyle the first time he was on him, flicking his hand out as Kyle tried to use the same crossover move he'd been punishing Dave with, slapping the ball away, beating Kyle to it, then lofting a pass toward the Knights' basket almost in the same motion.

For a moment it might have looked like a pass to no one. Except that Pedro knew better. Pedro had heard Joe say "hey" even before Pedro had control of the ball, and Pedro knew that meant one thing: He had taken off like a wide receiver on a fly pattern.

So as the ball came down near their free throw line at the other end of the court, there was Joe coming hard from the right, ahead of the field, collecting the ball in stride, taking one dribble, and laying the ball in.

One stop, two easy points, just like that.

First stop of the day, Pedro told himself, *but not my last.*

Because nobody was stopping him today.

• • •

He was so locked in on Kyle Sullivan he nearly followed him to the Warriors locker room at halftime. By then the Knights were ahead by a basket.

When they came back out on the floor, Coach Cory told Pedro he was starting the second half with the first unit.

"You know I always ride with the hot man on offense," Coach said. "Well, today I'm doing the same thing on defense."

Kyle would get loose sometimes in the third quarter, but it would take a screen to do it, sometimes more than one screen on the same play. And even then, Pedro was able to get around the screens and stay with his man, reading what he was doing like he was a book he'd read already.

Pedro knew when to give him room and when to get up on him. It was why what was usually the Warriors' one-two punch had become one guy: Nate Clark.

Nate was single-handedly keeping the game close, working mostly against Jeff, sometimes against Bobby, and sometimes against Clarence.

When Nate made his last three shots of the third quarter and his first two in the fourth, Coach Cory finally decided, almost in desperation, to put Ned Hancock on him, to see if he could cool him off or at least slow him down.

Even Ned couldn't.

Nate stayed hot and with four minutes left, the game was tied at 40–all. Usually Ned could shut anybody down, at any position. Use his length the way he had used it that day in practice against Pedro. But today, his length, even all his great basketball instincts were no match for Nate Clark's quickness.

Pedro's dad always said that the only way to beat speed in sports was with more speed. Ned didn't have that and Nate was beating him as effortlessly as he had the other guys.

With two minutes to go and the game still tied, Coach Cory called time-out. He was switching Pedro over to guard Nate.

"No," Ned said.

His face was red and he was breathing hard.

Pedro couldn't believe it: The kid who never

looked tired, who never even seemed to *sweat,* was gassed now.

He just won't admit it, Pedro thought.

"Ned," Coach said. "Listen to me." It was amazing. Even now it was as if he had to negotiate with Ned Hancock. "The kid's just having one of those unconscious days. It's nobody's fault. I'm not sure even *I* could guard him today. And we're gonna need your energy on offense the rest of the way. You all know how much I preach defense, from day one. But this thing has turned into a shoot-out, which means we gotta keep scoring the basketball."

"Coach, I *got* him!" Ned said. "I can do it all."

He never seemed to raise his voice, on the basketball court or anywhere else. Too cool. But Pedro was pretty sure everybody in the gym had heard him now.

Pedro wondered what it must be like, to actually believe that about yourself. Not just believe it, but come out and say it.

Coach Cory let him stay on Nate. But right

away Nate got loose for a dribble-drive, pulling up just inside the free throw line the way he had the entire game, making one of those one-handed teardrop shots.

Now the Warriors were ahead, 48–46.

Ned let Pedro bring the ball up, even though he usually did that at the end of games, no matter who was playing point guard for the Knights.

Then Pedro was the one getting inside his man, getting into the lane the way Nate just had at the other end, going up as if he were shooting before twisting his body just enough in midair to fire a pass to Ned on the baseline.

Ned was ten feet away from the basket and if he had one shot he liked the best, this was it.

Only he seemed to short-arm this one a little. Pedro watched the ball in the air and from his angle, it looked short. And it was. But Ned had enough spin on the ball and enough touch and it caught just enough of the front of the rim to give it a chance.

Pedro held his breath as he watched the ball bounce up, come down on the back of the rim, and catch a piece of the backboard before finally dropping through.

Shooter's roll if there ever was one.

48–all.

Under a minute now. Pedro couldn't even remember the last time he felt this good—this *happy*—on a basketball court. However this game came out.

He was a point guard again.

Problem was, he was the point guard who should have been the one trying to shut down Nate Clark. As soon as the Warriors had the ball back, Nate not only got open for a fifteen-footer, but Ned foolishly fouled him as he was making the shot. When Nate made the foul shot, too, it put the Warriors up by three.

Thirty seconds to play.

As Pedro started to bring the ball up the court, he looked over, thinking Coach Cory might want to call time-out. Coach just told him to push the sucker up, get the first good shot they saw.

It belonged to Jeff. Maybe the Warriors thought Pedro would want to bang the ball down low to Ned again, but he faked the pass to Ned, threw it over to Jeff on the left wing, and watched as he buried a jumper from the left side.

The Knights were down by a point, 51–50.

Pedro knew what to do next without Coach saying a word. Just because point guards were supposed to know. He didn't even hesitate in the frontcourt as soon as Nate was foolish enough to give the ball up, passing it to Kyle.

Pedro fouled right away, going for the ball, not wanting to get tagged with an intentional foul. All Kyle was going to get, now that the Knights were over the foul limit, was the chance to shoot a one-and-one.

He had to make the first foul shot to get the second.

Kyle, who hadn't taken a single shot in the fourth quarter, missed. Joe grabbed the rebound. Now Coach Cory called time-out, the Knights still down by one on the day when they had a chance to be the first team in two years to beat the Wilton Warriors.

In the huddle, Coach Cory said to Pedro and Ned, "Just run that little two-man game we used to run last year. Get Ned a good look down there in the low blocks, and send a bunch of sad faces back to Wilton."

"Sounds like a plan," Pedro said.

They spread the court. Pedro burned some clock, made it look as if he might go back to Jeff, and ended up with Ned on the right side. Ned faked as if he was going to set a pick on Kyle Sullivan, tore down toward the basket, and ended up wide open in his money spot.

Eight seconds.

Kyle saw what was happening and took off for Ned, but he wasn't going to get there in time.

Ned hesitated when he got the ball, but it shouldn't have mattered, because he had enough height on Kyle to shoot over him all day long.

Five seconds, Pedro saw.

Shoot it.

Ned released the ball.

Only he hadn't shot it. Instead, he wheeled and threw a dart back over to Pedro, now open on the left wing.

Three seconds.

Nothing for Pedro to do but catch and shoot, or the game was going to end without the Knights ever putting the ball in the air.

Inside his head was his dad's voice, telling him to trust it.

He let the ball go in time, felt as if he'd put a good stroke on it, even though he hadn't attempted an outside shot all day. In the air, the ball looked as if it was on line and had a chance, but he had put a little too much on it, tried to make too sure, and it hit off the back of the rim and bounced toward the left corner as the horn sounded ending the game.

The Knights had lost by a point, lost their first game of the season, lost their chance to knock off Wilton.

Lost because the best shooter they had had passed up a wide-open shot to pass the ball to a guy he knew couldn't make a shot to save his life these days.

Me, Pedro thought.

FIFTEEN

Pedro knew that even if he did say something to Ned, Ned would have the perfect answer: What's the problem, dude? You were open.

Coach always said that if a teammate was more open than you, pass him the ball, and that's exactly what Ned had done.

Except.

Except he never passed the ball back out when he got the ball down there, which is why the last thing in the world Pedro had expected was to be hoisting up a buzzer-beater.

It was bad enough that he'd missed, and they'd blown a sweet opportunity to beat Wilton. What was even worse, what hurt Pedro even more, was to think that Ned Hancock, the ultimate team guy, had decided today he'd rather mess with Pedro's head a little more than beat the Wilton Warriors.

"This thing is officially messed up," Joe said.

"You figured that out, huh?" Pedro said.

They were in town an hour after the game, having finished up with their shakes and fries at Bobby Van's, the diner all the kids in town liked the best. Now they were just walking around until Joe's mom picked them up in a little while.

"You gotta do something about this," Joe said. "*We* gotta do something about it." They had stopped in front of the video store. Joe wanted to go in there and rent a game for when they got home. "I could say something if you want."

"I told you, I'm going to."

"When?"

"This week."

"Can you at least tell me what you're going to say?"

"You'll see."

"What's that mean?"

"It means you'll see."

"I still don't get why this has to be such a big secret."

"It's not a secret," Pedro said, grinning. "Not to me, anyway."

"But you don't care to share."

Pedro said, "Hey, I already shared half of my fries."

Joe went inside the video store. Pedro told him to go ahead and pick something out, he'd meet him in a few minutes in front of Casa Luis, where Joe's mom was picking them up.

When Pedro got to his dad's restaurant, he didn't walk in right away, as cold as it was outside. Instead he stood off to the side of the front window, snuck a look through it, and saw that his dad was in there by himself, having come right back to work as soon as the Wilton game was over.

Luis Morales was standing on a chair, carefully taking down a huge painting from one of the back walls, the painting almost too big for him to wrap his arms around. Somehow he managed, gently laying the painting on the floor before he hopped down, picked it up again and carried it toward the front.

As heavy as the painting clearly was, Pedro could see his dad smiling.

Just then, Joe and his mom pulled up in her car, Joe calling out and asking if he was ready to go. Pedro told him he'd call him later, for now he was going to stay and help his dad do some work.

He walked through the front door, amazed at how much it was starting to look like a real restaurant, even with boxes still stacked in front of the bar.

"To what do I owe this honor?" his dad said.

"I heard you were short good workers lately," Pedro said.

"Only for a little while," his dad said. "Then some friends of mine showed up in their spare time to help me out."

"Mom says Mr. Miller turned out to be a bad sport."

Even the mention of Mr. Miller, Pedro saw, couldn't knock the smile off his dad's face. Maybe nothing would ever be able to do that inside Casa Luis.

"There are a lot of bad sports in the world," his dad said. "You just don't expect it from somebody who was supposed to be your friend."

You can say that again, Pedro thought.

"How do you handle it when that happens?" he asked his dad.

"Just keep playing your game, son." He reached over and mussed Pedro's thick hair, thick as his own. "Now, are you here to work or to talk?"

"Both," Pedro said.

It turned out the boxes, packed so carefully, with lots of padding, were full of dinner plates that his dad had ordered special all the way from California. Together they brought them to the kitchen one by one, set them in front of the shelves where Pedro's dad wanted them stacked, shelves Pedro knew his dad had painted himself after his painter had quit on him.

"I'm so scared I'm going to drop something," Pedro said.

"Trust it!" his dad yelled, and both of them laughed.

When they were done they moved some photographs around on the walls until his dad had all the walls in the place looking exactly the way he wanted them to. Then Pedro held the ladder in place while his dad climbed up and fixed his big ceiling fan.

Somehow it was work that felt like play, Pedro feeling the way he did when they were on the soccer field together. The only difference here was that he wasn't seeing the little boy inside his dad, he was seeing the great man that boy had become.

Nobody had been able to stop him, and now his grand opening was less than two weeks away.

When they had finished all their jobs, the two of them sitting at the bar where his dad already had the cash register and computer and credit card machine set up, Pedro said, "I'm proud of you, Papa."

"I haven't done anything yet."

"Yes," Pedro said, "you have."

"It was a long journey to my dream."

Pedro said, "Everything you had to go through to get here—was it worth it?"

"Look around you," his dad said, making a sweeping gesture with his arm that seemed to take in the whole place at once. "What do you think?"

"I don't think, Papa. I *know.*"

Luis Morales looked at his son. Then he placed one hand over his heart, reached out with the other and touched Pedro's.

"If you know in your heart that you're right," he said, "then nothing—and nobody—can beat you."

He wrapped Pedro up in a hug, the two of them so tight to each other Pedro felt as if his dad had put their two hearts together. Pedro was sure in that moment, as sure as he could be about anything, that nobody was going to beat him either.

SIXTEEN

They called it a debate at Vernon Middle School, but it really wasn't.

Both candidates would give their speeches, and then they'd each have the option to respond to the other candidate's speech for an additional minute—what they knew from Social Studies was called a rebuttal.

"I look at it this way, after the way Ned's been acting toward you," Sarah had said at lunch. "At least he'll be putting the *butt* back in rebuttal."

That one even got a grin out of Joe. After Sarah said it, he made a motion like he was shooting an imaginary basketball, held the finish and said, "Sarah. From downtown."

Pedro had spent all last night working on his speech, delivering it over and over again in a quiet voice in his room, not wanting his parents to hear, not wanting to have them find out his secret this close to the election. He kept reading the speech until he felt he had it memorized, then repeated it a few times standing in front of the mirror in his bathroom, finally even managing to look at himself without giggling.

When he felt he had it down cold, he called Sarah and recited it to her from memory, timing himself as he did, proud that he'd brought it in a few seconds under three minutes, which was going to be the time limit.

When he'd finished with Sarah there had been total silence at the other end of the phone, as if the line had gone dead.

"Well?" he said finally.

Sarah said, "It's perfect."

"You're nice, but you're wrong," he said. "It's not. But it's all I've got. Or maybe all I am."

"No," Sarah said, "you're the one who's wrong. It's great, it really is."

"I was waiting for you to say that you couldn't have done better yourself."

In her serious voice Sarah said, "I couldn't have even come close."

Pedro hadn't said a word to Ned, not one, since the end of the Wilton game. When they'd seen each other in class, or passed each other in the hall, all they would do is give each other the nod.

Even today, Pedro didn't say anything when they were up on the stage and had taken their places facing each other from individual podiums. They hadn't even gone through the motion of shaking hands.

Mr. Lucchino was with them on the stage, holding his own microphone. He produced an antique silver dollar from his pocket, holding it up to the crowd, and told Pedro he could make the call.

He said *heads* into his microphone and Mr. Lucchino picked the coin off the floor and said heads it was. It meant Pedro could decide whether he wanted to go first or not.

"I'll go second," he said.

"Then I guess you're up, Mr. Hancock," Mr. Lucchino said. "You've got three minutes."

Pedro had been wondering where Ned's speech was, thought maybe he was keeping it folded up in his pocket until the last possible moment. There was no paper in his hands, no paper on the podium in front of him, no nothing, making Pedro think that maybe Ned had memorized his own speech so well he didn't even need a copy in case he lost his place.

But as soon as he started, Pedro realized that Ned hadn't prepared a speech. He was clearly making it up as he went along.

"You guys all know me, right?" he said, not looking at Pedro, turning toward the audience instead. Pedro could see Jeff Harmon and Dave DeLuca in the front row. "And if you do, you probably know that I pretty much have been captain of every team I've ever played on."

He paused for a second, letting that sink in. "I've never had to run for captain, it's just that the other guys on the team always thought *I* was the best guy for the job."

For some reason, Jeff and Dave applauded

now, even though nobody else in the auditorium did. Ned smiled at them and made a time-out gesture with his hands, stopping them.

"I actually feel a little funny being up here," Ned said, "because I've never been very comfortable talking about myself. I've always preferred to let my actions speak louder than my words."

Tell me about it, Pedro thought.

He was waiting for Ned to talk about what kind of difference he could make as class president, but instead Ned started talking about sports. As if they were in the gym and not in the auditorium, as if being a difference-maker in a basketball game made him the best guy for the job. So he talked about some of the games he'd won and the teams he'd played on, almost like someone reading stuff off the back of his own baseball card.

As he did, Pedro checked the runners' watch his parents had given him on his last birthday, one he hardly ever wore but had put on today. He planned to take it off and just put it down in front of him when he started speaking, not wanting Mr. Lucchino to have to tell him he'd run over his allotted time.

Still a minute to go for Ned, he saw.

Only Ned was wrapping things up, coming up on what he must have thought was going to be a big finish.

There wasn't one.

"I'm not here to talk bad about Pedro, or talk up myself," he said. "I'm just looking to be captain of the school this time. Everybody else seems to think I'm the *man*." He paused there, and smiled, like that was one line he *had* prepared. "The man for the job, I mean. I hope you guys do, too."

Jeff and Dave stood up, clapping their hands hard. Everyone else applauded along with them. But Pedro noticed that Jeff and Dave were the only ones standing.

Mr. Lucchino said, "Your turn, Mr. Morales."

He got out of his chair now, because it was finally time to say everything that needed to be said.

This had been Pedro's plan all along. He wasn't going to say what needed to be said in the gym.

He was going to say it here.

All he changed from the night before was his opening line.

"I've never been the *man*," Pedro said. "Just a team man."

He was off. Not feeling nervous. Not rushing it. Feeling like he was exactly where he was supposed to be, the way he always had in basketball, at least until this season.

"This isn't a contest about which one of us is the better athlete, because if it was, Ned wouldn't just be elected president of Vernon Middle, he'd be elected mayor of Vernon."

That got a laugh.

From everyone, it sounded like.

Pedro wasn't looking out in the audience, though.

He was looking directly at Ned Hancock.

"You know who I am," he said in a clear, loud voice. "You know I never pretend to be something I'm not. That I would never pretend to be somebody's friend and then act in a way opposite of that."

He paused again, picked out a face in the audience the way Sarah had told him to. Her face. Then he turned right back to Ned. But as soon as Pedro's eyes were back on him, Ned quickly turned away, the kid who was supposed to be the coolest in the whole school not looking so cool at all.

Pedro had always thought of Ned Hancock as being so much bigger than he was.

Not now.

Now they were even.

"If I'm on your side," Pedro said, "you don't have to keep looking around to see if I'm still there. Because I will *always* be there."

This time he had to pause because his classmates were applauding. For a moment, he wished his father could be here. Hearing this. Seeing this.

When they stopped, he started in again.

"I will be exactly the same kind of president I am as a teammate," he said. "I will always give myself up for the good of the team. I will always be looking for ways to make us better. I will never do anything to make any one of you look bad. I don't just want people to look at us and say we're one of the best schools in Vernon. I want them to say we're *the* best. Because we are."

More applause, like the other sixth-graders were really getting into it now.

He looked into the audience again and caught Sarah's eye. She smiled at him and he smiled back and didn't care who noticed.

"I'm not doing this for me," Pedro said. "Because that's not me. I don't think I'm better than everybody else. I just want to bring out the best in everybody else."

Sarah made a little fist, knowing he was close to the end now.

"I know candidates are supposed to make a lot of promises," he said, "but I've only got one: If I'm for you I'll never be against you. I've never been the biggest star. Just the best teammate you could ever have. Thank you very much."

Sarah was the first one to jump to her feet,

halfway between the stage and the gym doors. Then Joe was up with her, and Bobby and Jamal. Then the whole audience was standing, Pedro noticing that Jeff and Dave were the last two to get up.

When it finally got quiet again, Mr. Lucchino said, "Would you care to rebut, Mr. Hancock?"

Ned shook his head.

"I'm done," he said.

SEVENTEEN

The next game with Wilton was the day after the debate. If you could even call it a debate, Joe kept saying.

"Looked more like a beatdown to me," he said.

"I did okay," Pedro said.

"Yeah," he said, "like the Spurs did okay in the Finals when they swept LeBron four straight."

The election would be held Monday. Normally, Pedro would have been all fixed on that, worrying it to death all weekend. But now here came the Wilton Warriors again, in the gym at Wilton High. Here was a chance for them to even the score right away for the way the last game between them had ended, Pedro missing that shot at the buzzer.

He'd worry about the election when the game was over.

Coach Cory went with their regular starting lineup, what Pedro was sure now would be the regular starting lineup the rest of the season unless somebody got hurt:

Ned, Joe, Jeff, Dave, Jamal.

In the huddle right before the game started, it almost seemed as if he'd prepared what he wanted to say to them the way Pedro had prepared his speech for the debate.

"We're winning this game today," he said. "We're winning the *championship* of today. We're winning because we're not going to let them go through another season undefeated. We're winning because we're not letting them think from now to the playoffs that they got our number. 'Cause they don't. 'Cause when we play Knights basketball we're the best. So that's all I'm asking you to do today: Don't play *your* game. Play *our* game. 'Cause it's not gonna be just one of you beating them today on their own dang court. It's gonna be all of you."

I hope, Pedro thought.

And it sure looked like a total team effort at the start when Joe Sutter, of all people, was left wide-open because of double-teams on Ned, and Joe promptly made the two longest outside shots he'd made all year.

Just like that, the Knights were ahead, 4–0.

Dave DeLuca, maybe just going on pride, was doing a much better job on Kyle Sullivan than last game. Kyle was getting his points, and so was Nate Clark. But they had to work to get them, and knew they were going to have to keep working and keep scoring to stay in the game.

Because as soon as Joe stopped shooting, Ned started.

And in the first half, he could not miss.

He couldn't miss even when he was off-balance a little, or didn't seem to have the best look at the basket. Or had a hand in his face. Didn't matter whether they were double-teaming him or not. Pedro had never seen him this hot, or shooting this much. Coach might have said it wasn't just going to be one of them today, but right now that's exactly the way it was.

It was Ned against the world.

Being the man.

Coach left him in with the second unit, but Pedro just did what Dave had been doing when Dave was at the point, which meant giving Ned the ball and just getting out of the way.

At the half, the Knights were ahead, 36–24.

Ned had twenty of the Knights' points.

"It's like he's trying to prove some kind of point," Joe said to Pedro.

"Yeah," Pedro said. "*Lots* of points."

For this one half of basketball the guy Pedro used to think was the ultimate team guy had become a one-man team. But nobody on the Knights was complaining one bit, mostly because it was sure working for them.

Until Ned went cold.

He had briefly come out passing at the start of the third quarter, maybe as a way of throwing the Warriors off. But Jeff missed a wide-open look and then missed another after Ned had drawn most of the coverage to himself. Jamal missed one in the lane, a wide-open layup. In the same stretch Kyle hit two fast baskets for the Warriors, then made a couple of free throws, Dave having fouled him as he went for a third.

Just like that, the lead was cut in half, only two minutes into the quarter. Suddenly the Knights were playing tight. Not only had the momentum of the game changed, but you could see the Warriors feeding off it. After Nate got loose for a couple of easy baskets, the Knights were only ahead by two.

Usually Ned could change the momentum of a game all by himself, by the force of his own game. Just not today. His shooting touch was gone.

He had torched the kid guarding him, Josh Watson, the whole first half, but now Josh was dogging him all over the court, putting a hand on him off the ball sometimes just to annoy him—and it was working. Ned kept missing.

The Warriors were up a basket. Coach Cory put Pedro back in with two minutes left in the quarter, telling him to get everybody back involved in the dang game. But no matter how much he tried to swing the ball, once it got to Ned, it stopped, nearly every time.

Ned was pressing now, forcing shots, like he was letting everybody know he was going to shoot his way out of this, no matter what.

Only he couldn't. He kept missing. It was why Coach Cory finally took him out at the start of the fourth quarter, saying he wanted to give him a rest. But as cold as Ned had been, the Knights still looked lost with him on the bench, and the Warriors quickly built their lead to eight.

Coach Cory knew he had no choice, and after a couple of minutes that he hoped had cleared Ned's head, he put his star right back in the game. Trouble was, Ned really had needed the rest. And still needed it. He had tried playing one-on-five for way too much of the game and now it wasn't just that he'd lost his shooting touch, he'd lost his legs, too.

Even with that, the rest of the guys on the floor treated him like their best option.

He was the man for them even when he wasn't.

There were four minutes left when Coach Cory came down to where Pedro was sitting. The Knights were down by ten now, and fading fast.

"You're the only one I have who can do this," he said to Pedro.

"Do what?"

"Turn us back into a team." He smiled. "Go save him and go save us."

Nate was getting ready to shoot two free throws when Pedro subbed in. Before he did, Pedro quickly called everybody around him.

Ned had been trying to send Pedro a message all season. Now it was Pedro's turn.

"Five playing as one the rest of the way," he said. "Five as one. Now let's *do* this."

Nate made one of two free throws. Wilton was up eleven, 53–42.

That was when the Knights made their stand. Joe got a wide-open look at a three-pointer and buried it after Pedro barked at him to shoot. Then Pedro stole the ball from Kyle Sullivan and fed a streaking Jamal for an easy layup.

53–47.

Just like that, the momentum was back with

the Knights, as if someone had thrown a switch. Pedro could feel it, he knew his teammates could feel it. They were the ones playing with energy now, the best kind of basketball energy there was:

Five playing as one.

Nate forced a jumper that missed by a lot. Joe grabbed the rebound and fed Pedro, who dribbled down the court and broke free in the lane, looking to feed either Jamal or Ned. But when nobody stepped out on him, he ended up with a clear path to the basket. He laid the ball home.

53–49.

Now it was the Warriors who looked tired, who'd lost *their* legs. Kyle missed with a jumper. Joe grabbed another rebound and fired an outlet pass to Pedro at midcourt. He had Ned cutting behind him, Jamal flying to catch up with them on Pedro's right.

Ned was the one with two good steps on his man, Josh Watson.

But instead of passing the ball to Ned as he cut to the basket, Pedro told him with his eyes to pull up on the wing for a three-pointer. As soon as he did, Pedro hit him with a sweet bounce pass.

Josh tried to catch up at the last second, thinking he could block the shot. But he was too late. Ned let the ball go, and even with Josh flailing at him and clipping him on his wrist, Pedro could see just from his release that he'd regained his form at the best possible time.

One ref put both arms up as soon as the ball went in, making it official that the shot was a three-pointer.

At almost the exact same moment, the other ref blew his whistle, calling a foul on Josh.

Ned didn't look at either one of them and didn't change expression—he just nodded. He walked to the line, took the ball, looked as cool as the Ned of old and made the free throw that made it a four-point play.

His first basket of the fourth quarter.

One minute left.

The Warriors called time-out. In the Knights huddle Coach Cory said, "I saved one more time-out for when they miss."

Not if they missed.

When.

Coach said to Pedro, "Can only be Kyle or Nate taking the shot. You got Kyle?"

"All day," Pedro said.

To Bobby Murray, Coach Cory said, "What about Nate the Great?"

"He's done," Bobby said, "like dinner."

Coming out of the time-out it looked like the Warriors might run the clock all the way down, since there was no shot clock in sixth-grade basketball. But they made their move with twenty seconds left.

Kyle had the ball up top. Pedro had been waiting for him to make his move and now he did. Pedro couldn't see what was happening behind him, but knew Nate had to be running around trying to shake free of Bobby. But he couldn't get open, because Bobby was all over him.

Kyle had to do something on his own.

He had started dribbling slowly to his right. Now he picked up the pace. The best move he had was ducking his shoulder and going around the corner, just using a burst of speed to beat you off the dribble, leaving you in the dust.

Only Pedro was ready for it, overplaying him, knowing Kyle didn't like going to his left. Pedro beat him to the sideline, planted his foot there, which meant Kyle had to reverse the ball or get rid of it.

With time running out on him.

Had to be under fifteen seconds now.

For one moment, Kyle tried to look everywhere at once, at Pedro, at Nate, at the clock. As soon as he did, he dribbled the ball off his foot.

Out of bounds.

"Off him!" Kyle yelled to the ref, pointing at Pedro.

The ref grinned at him. "Only if he's wearing one of your sneakers, son."

Twelve seconds left.

Pedro called the Knights' last time-out.

It had taken longer than it was supposed to. A lot had happened in just a handful of games. But Pedro was finally where he wanted to be.

EIGHTEEN

When Coach Cory started talking in the huddle, he was talking only to Pedro and Ned.

"Seems to me that for a couple of knuckleheaded sixth-graders," he said, grinning as he did, "that you've always had options on top of options for those pick-and-rolls of yours. Just pick the one you like best now."

They both nodded.

To Joe and Jamal and Bobby, Coach Cory said, "Joe, you clear out over to the left wing. Bobby, you're up top. Jamal, you move around in the lane—just don't clog it up if you see somebody comin' your way."

Now Coach Cory spoke to all of them. "We clear?"

They all nodded.

He put his hand out and they put theirs in on top of it.

"You know all the fun I'm always talking about in basketball? Well, this here is that fun."

The horn sounded. As they started walking back on the court, Ned grabbed Pedro by the arm. "I've been messing up," he said. "Big-time."

"You just missed a bunch of shots you usually make," Pedro said.

"I'm not just talking about today," Ned said. "I've been a jerk."

Pedro grinned. "We can debate *that* another time. Right now, let's just win the game."

"Got a plan?" Ned said.

"Yeah," Pedro said. "We outwork their butts."

"Pick-and-roll without the pick?" Ned said.

"Thought you'd never ask."

They pounded fists. The refs were taking a little extra time, because something was wrong with the scoreboard. While they straightened it out at the scorers' table, Pedro got between Joe and Bobby and told them what the plan was.

Joe said, "Are you insane?"

"Probably."

Joe nodded. "I'm good with that," he said to Pedro.

Pedro knew what was going to happen. He could see it inside his head. Could see it happening like his dad making that bicycle kick of his, putting the ball in the net every single time, one move leading to the next.

And to the next.

Jamal inbounded the ball at half-court. Pedro went and got it, as Joe and Jamal and Bobby cleared out. Kyle was on Pedro, and Josh Watson was still on Ned as Ned came running toward Pedro, looking for all the world like he wanted to set a huge pick.

Josh called it out.

Pedro didn't care. He knew what was coming the way Ned did, because they were back to reading each other's minds the way they used to.

It went exactly the way it had in the pickup game right before the season started. Ned stopped before he set his pick. Josh laid off him, giving him room, expecting him to break for the basket whether he'd set a pick or not.

Pedro checked the clock.

Eight seconds.

Instead of cutting for the basket, Ned popped back into the corner. When he was open, Pedro whipped the ball over to him.

As soon as he did, it wasn't just Josh covering him, it was Kyle running at him, too. Like the last game. It was the same spot where Ned had just made his three-pointer. The Warriors weren't going to leave him open from there.

When Ned saw the double-team, he kicked the ball right back to Pedro, wide-open now at the right of the foul line.

Wide-open for the same shot he'd missed against Wilton the other day.

Only they had more time today.

So *now* Ned cut down the baseline for the basket, hand up, calling for the ball. A step ahead of Josh Watson.

Ned was open, too. Just not enough.

Trust it, Pedro's dad always said.

Trust it.

So Pedro trusted that Joe Sutter, the real hot

hand today, was where he was supposed to be. Where Pedro had told him to be.

Pedro's eyes never left Ned as he one-handed a no-look pass all the way across the court to his best bud.

Then all he had to do was watch as Joe caught the ball and didn't hesitate. No time for that. He just squared his shoulders and let the ball go and watched along with everybody else as the shot that beat Wilton hit nothing but net.

Game.

NINETEEN

Election Day.

Everybody was scheduled to cast their ballots in their last morning class.

The teachers in each class would then collect the ballots and deliver them to Mr. Lucchino's office after the period. Then he and the vice principal, Mrs. Connolly, would count the votes while the students were at lunch.

The announcement about which ticket had won, Pedro's or Ned's, would come at two o'clock.

"It's like it's the end of a game," Pedro said, "but I don't get to do anything to decide how it comes out."

"You already did," Joe said.

"How do you figure?" Pedro said.

"When you made your speech, to me that was game, set and match," Joe said. "That's what they say in tennis, right?"

"Only when the match is over," Pedro said.

"Trust me," Joe said, "this baby is over."

He and Joe and Sarah all voted in Social Studies. Pedro smiled as he looked at his own name, then put a check mark next to it so big and thick he made the little box disappear.

When they got to the cafeteria, Ned was standing there.

Standing right next to one of the posters Sarah had made, this one with Pedro's class picture from last year on it, the message pretty basic: VOTE FOR PEDRO.

Ned pointed to it.

"I did," he said.

"Did what?"

Joe was already inside the cafeteria trying to find them seats.

"Voted for you," Ned Hancock said.

"No way."

"Way," he said. "It should be you. It always should have been you."

Pedro was glad he hadn't been this speech-less at the debate. All he could finally manage was, "Well, thanks."

Ned said, "I was so afraid I might lose at something that I forgot the way real winners are supposed to act."

Pedro started to say something but Ned held up a hand. "Let me finish, please," he said. "At least this is one speech I practiced."

Pedro waited.

"I finally figured out something I'd sort of known all along, even if I didn't want to admit it," Ned said. "Real winners act exactly like you."

He put out his fist, the way he had before the last play on Saturday against Wilton. Then he and Pedro grinned at each other and twisted their fists like they used to.

Twisting the lock.

"Like both of us," Pedro said.

It was a couple of minutes after two o'clock when they heard the school intercom come on. Pedro, Joe and Sarah were in a free period, the one they always got on Monday, trying to get a jump on their homework.

All day, Pedro had been trying to act as if he didn't care. But he did. He cared as much about this as anything that had ever happened to him in sports. In this moment, knowing that Mr. Lucchino was about to read the results, he knew he cared that much.

And more.

He sat there and waited along with the rest of the school as Mr. Lucchino said all the votes had been counted and re-counted and they had a result.

Pedro closed his eyes and couldn't help himself—there was his dad's face smiling at him, smiling the way Pedro knew he would smile if he could tell him tonight that he'd won.

If he won.

It was very quiet now in Mrs. Fusco's study hall. Pedro could hear Mr. Lucchino breathing into the microphone he kept on his desk.

Then he said, "I am pleased to announce that the president and vice president for this school year . . . are Pedro Morales and Sarah Layng. Congratulations to both of them."

And for the first time in his life, even more than when he'd finished his speech the other day, Pedro felt as if he could hear the whole school cheer.

For him.

Game, set, match.

TWENTY

It was the next weekend, Saturday morning, and Pedro told his dad that he didn't have to play soccer today, that he should rest up for the big opening of Casa Luis that night.

"I don't need rest," his dad said. "I need play."

So they had both put on their hoodies and grabbed their soccer balls and Luis Morales drove them over to Vernon Middle to play. As if it were any other Saturday.

But they both knew differently.

As they stretched on the cold grass, Luis Morales repeated something he'd been repeating over and over again all week.

"I still can't believe you kept a secret that big from me," he said.

Meaning the election.

"I think keeping that secret from you and Mom was harder than beating Ned," Pedro said. "But I did it, Papa. I did it."

"You've done it all," his dad said. "Including winning back your starting job."

Pedro had found out the night after the election—Coach Cory pulled him aside before practice. So it was like a double celebration when he'd gotten home, for the point guard and the class president. His mom even bought an ice cream cake for the occasion.

When he'd blown out the one candle on top of the cake, his mom had told him how proud she was, not that he'd won, but that he'd put himself out there the way he had. Then his dad had hugged him hard, tears in his eyes, and said, "This is a week when all our dreams have come true. Even the ones I didn't know about until today."

So finally it was the day of the opening, a special soccer Saturday if there ever was one. Tomorrow Pedro would make his first start of the season for the Knights.

As they finished stretching, the sun came out. Like the morning sun was smiling down on the two Morales men, father and son.

Luis Morales began to play with the ball now, one foot and then the other, the ball bouncing straight up off one knee, then the other knee, then off his head.

"The only thing I'm sorry about," Pedro said, "is that you didn't get to hear my speech."

His dad caught the ball out of the air now, put it on his hip, and said to Pedro, "So let me hear it now."

"Here?" Pedro said.

"Right here and right now," his dad said. "Think about all the times when you listened to your papa give his speech about America. It's about time I listened to you."

Pedro talked to his dad then the way he had talked to his classmates. Talked about doing what was best for everybody, talked about trust, talked about looking for the best in each other.

He remembered every single word.

By heart.

When he finished, his dad hugged him again,

then picked him up like he wanted to lift him to the sky. This time he didn't make Pedro shout out "President Morales" the way he had at the start of it all. He just whispered these two words into his ear:

"My son."

Then Luis Morales placed his soccer ball on the ground and kicked it as far as he could, as if trying to kick it all the way to the front door of Casa Luis, and told Pedro he'd race him to it.

Father and son took off then, running and laughing at the same time, as if chasing their dreams together, as if you could no longer tell their dreams apart.

Turn the page for a preview
of Mike Lupica's next novel,

ONE

Jake Stuart was the man now.

Oh yeah, *definitely* the man, playing the only position he ever wanted to play, center mid, feeling like the center of everything now, the whole game going through him.

Breaking into the clear at midfield, plenty of green in front of him, dribbling the ball like a total pro, like one of his heroes, the ball on a string with both feet, Jake feeling the way he always did in moments like these, as if the field were tilting away from him.

As if he were running downhill.

Jake thought: *Please let everybody stay onside. Wingers, strikers, everybody.*

Please just wait for me this one time.

No whistles.

That was all the help he was going to need. He'd already made up his mind that somehow, whatever it took, he was going to figure out a way to take it all the way, that he was going to score himself this time.

He just hadn't let anybody else in on his little secret, at least not yet.

Jake totally loved this part, running in the open field even before he got into the box, before things got a lot more crowded, like somebody had shrunk the huge field to something that felt like the inside of a school bus. Jake loved the moment—a moment at full speed—when you started to make something happen, when you turned defense into offense all by yourself.

Coach Lord called Jake his "coach on the field."

All game long, the center mid for Lincoln's twelve-year-old travel team had been coming up hard on Jake when he'd try to make any kind of play. The other kid had figured out early that if he could be aggressive with Jake, knock him off the ball first chance he got, before Jake got a head of steam going for him, that Jake's team—Belmont—

had hardly any chance of pushing the ball, forcing the action, in any kind of serious way.

Smart kid.

One who knew that if he could force Jake to pass before he wanted to, that Lincoln's outside guys could shut down the play every single time, pick Jake's teammates clean.

And just like that, Jake would be back on defense, throwing his own game into reverse, knowing he had to help out the guys behind him. Even with all the help he was supposed to have behind him on defense, stoppers and sweepers and fullbacks set up like a defensive backfield in football, Jake still felt a little bit like it was him against the world.

But Lincoln's center mid hung back this time.

Maybe it was because he was just gassed by now. Maybe he was being lazy, assuming this would be another time when Jake was going to give the ball up early, even this late in the game.

Whatever.

Didn't matter.

Jake had room to maneuver now.

Like finally having room to breathe.

The big scoreboard at Belmont Middle School

was behind him, on the parking lot end of the field, but Jake knew there had been thirty seconds left when he started up the field.

Plenty of time, he told himself. His ball now. For the last seconds of this game, *his* game.

At last.

Quinn O'Dell, Jake's best friend on the team, Belmont's goalie, always said that Jake didn't just have eyes in back of his head, he had them on both sides of his head, too. Sometimes Jake really felt as if he did. It was why he knew, just *knew* as he slowed down a little, that his guys weren't offsides, that they hadn't gone too far ahead of the play and behind the last Lincoln defender. Cal Morris was running a step behind over on his right, and his left middie, Matt Purcell, was farther behind than that to Jake's left. He knew that because Matt was the one who'd been acting gassed the whole second half.

Jake knew all that the way he knew what was going to happen at the end of this play. What was going to happen was that he was going to put the ball behind the Lincoln goalie. Control things right until the ball was behind that hot dog.

Finally—*finally*—this was the way it was supposed to be, the way things were supposed to work out for him in the last minute of a game.

Jake saw it all: Their center mid laying back, the outside guys inching up anyway, as if Jake were going to pass it to Cal or Matt just by force of habit. Give it up for the team one more time.

Only sometimes, especially this close to the end, the best way to be a team guy was to score the goal.

Seemed like a plan.

Jake moved the ball to his left foot, which usually meant a pass to Cal on the right. The Lincoln kid, a tall redhead, face full of freckles, forgot about making the sliding-tackle move he'd been making on Jake the whole game, and flashed to his left thinking he could pick the pass off himself.

Only Jake kept the ball on his left foot, moved into that extra gear he had, that he'd *always* had, and went flying past the redhead. He saw him slip and fall out of the corner of his eye.

Jake against their sweeper now.

Their free safety. The gambler on the Lincoln team. This guy wasn't laying back, wasn't hesitating. He was coming right at Jake. But Jake put one of his favorite moves on him, nearly coming to a stop even though he'd been going at full speed, and put the ball behind him as he did, just for an instant. Reached back with his left leg like he was using it to shut a door behind him, like he was making a behind-the-back pass to himself, and just absolutely dusted the guy as he went right.

Money.

Just Jake and the goalie now.

This was the goalie who'd been talking nonstop since the game began. Talking to his teammates, to the refs, to the Belmont players, to his coach, even to his buddies in the stands. One of those guys. Coming way up into the field even when he didn't have to, showing off constantly, making flashier plays than he needed to make—how much did Jake hate that?—making hey-look-at-me saves and heaves and kicks and dives.

Another one on the Lincoln team who wasn't going to hang back. Wasn't his style. And this guy was *all* style. He wasn't going to be looking for his defense to bail him out, somehow get back into the play, somehow get between him and Jake.

You could see by the look on his face that this was the way he wanted it, the way it was, the way Jake wanted it:

Me against you.

Jake knew that eventually, even in team sports, it always came down to that in the end. He had always been a team man in soccer, from the beginning, but in sports you always looked for the moment when it was man-on-man, one-on-one, your best against his.

From the time Jake first started watching sports on television, he'd heard football announcers talking about how quarterbacks didn't really make it in the NFL until the game slowed down for them, until they could sit back there in the pocket and feel as if the play developing in front of them were in slow motion.

Jake felt that way now, even though he was flying, even though he'd made guys on the other team go flying past him.

Pick your spot, his mom had always told him, from the first time they were kicking the ball around in the backyard and the goal was the area between two stakes in the fence around the swimming pool.

Pick your spot unless the goalie commits first.

Most of all, don't rush.

Jake wasn't rushing.

Had to be around ten seconds left now.

Still time for him to beat this guy once and for all.

End the day right against this goalie, with his shirt that had more colors than Baskin-Robbins had flavors, with his bright red gloves and even his baseball cap turned around in a hot dog way.

The goalie clapped those red gloves now, eyeballing Jake the whole time, as if to say *bring it*.

In the words of Quinn O'Dell, who had a language all his own, the goalie was thuggin' on Jake to the end.

Jake didn't care.

Upper right corner.

That's where he was going with the shot.

But the goalie, no dope, was thinking right along with him, leaning that way.

Cake, Jake thought.

The kid had committed just enough, made up Jake's mind for him.

He could feel pressure coming now, feel the

crowd that should have been there earlier coming from behind and from the sides. But no way they were getting there in time. Jake planted his left foot, gave the ball one last small push to the outside, like he was teeing the sucker up.

Then he let it go.

For one shaky moment he thought he'd leaned back and got too far under it, that it might go sailing over the crossbar. And how many times had Jake seen that happen, a shooter alone in the box, all set up, getting too amped up and sending it deep into the woods?

Not this time.

The best part, the very best part, was that the Lincoln goalie was *so* sure of himself to the end. He was going to dazzle everybody with one more save, launch himself one last time like he was auditioning to get himself into SportsCenter's Top 10 Plays.

He had cheated a step to his left, shifting his weight, ready to pounce.

But Jake had put one last fake on the guy. The goalie went one way as the ball went the other. It wasn't just the ball Jake had on a string now, it was like he'd turned the goalie into a puppet that he'd flung to the side.

The ball tucked itself into the top corner, the strings of the net making Jake feel as if he'd swished one in hoops, as neatly as a hand fitting into a glove.

Goal.

But Jake didn't celebrate, didn't run around the way guys in other sports did at times like this, as if they've forgotten what the scoreboard said.

Jake hadn't forgotten.

Jake turned and took one last look at that scoreboard now, just because he couldn't make himself look anywhere else from where he stood on the field.

Visitors 7, Belmont 1.

It felt like the longest game of Jake's life.

And it was only the first game of the season.

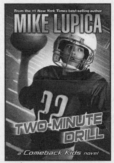